Lock Down Publications and Ca$h
Presents

I0637446

Bloodline of a
Savage II
Revelations

By
Prince A. Tauhid

First Edition 2024

Printed in the United States of America

This is a work of fiction. Names, characters, places, and incidents either are products of the author's imagination or are used fictitiously. Any similarity to actual events or locales or persons, living or dead, is entirely coincidental.

Lock Down Publications
P.O. Box 944
Stockbridge, GA 30281
www.lockdownpublications.com

Like our page on Facebook: Lock Down Publications
www.facebook.com/lockdownpublications.ldp

Stay Connected with Us!

Text **LOCKDOWN** to 22828 to stay up-to-date with new releases, sneak peaks, contests and more…

Like our page on Facebook:
Lock Down Publications

Join Lock Down Publications/The New Era Reading Group

Visit our website:
www.lockdownpublications.com

Follow us on Instagram:
Lock Down Publications

Email Us: We want to hear from you!

PART ONE

PROLOGUE

September 2009...

The day was a Friday and the second week of the College Football Season. Also, Week 1 of the NFL regular season kicking was off the same weekend. Drip made it his business to have the grand opening of the new social spot he owned for the many sports fans who wanted an additional place to hangout. The Ozone Sports Bar and Grill was his newest and most celebrated business venture. And he had a lot of family members there to experience the occasion, without him.

Von's father—Hound Jr.—was now a free man once more. He and Lilly reconnected on a friendship basis and were looking forward to working their way back to something stronger. The both of them had of course been invited there together to The Ozone. So was Von and Kidada. Monyetta accompanied Von and a male friend tagged along with Kidada. He was a gay guy who went by the name, "Passion Fruit," Adrian Cooper was his actual name. Kidada didn't care too much for a boyfriend. At least not as much as she did for a female companion. Her bisexual appetite couldn't be so easily fulfilled. Besides, she valued and appreciated the intimate bond and deeply compassionate acquaintance she now maintained with Monyetta, of all people.

While in Atlantic City, she, Von, and Monyetta enjoyed a night of gambling and fun. Kidada and Monyetta made their way to the suite earlier than Von had. While in the shower together, the two ladies touched, kissed, and bathed one another. They established something that night. Outside of Von knowing anything. He had no clue.

Meanwhile at the grand opening, Monk had his main sweetheart with him—Ayonna, a friend of Monyetta's. Then there was Cold Heart with Monyetta's sister by his side—Tiona. And no doubt Drip had his Ivy League college heartthrob with him—Divida. So was a stalking dude somewhere in the crowd, looking to execute a hit. He carried a loaded gun that had bullets with a specific name on them. Drip committed a serious mistake. He'd forgotten to have metal detectors at the entrance, and the security on hand didn't check for weapons. Things were subject to get crazy. As they always did.

As Drip, Monk, Von, Cold Heart, Hound Jr, Lilly, Kidada, and other Savage family members where in the picture taking section posing for photos, the hitter weaved his way through a maze of people in attendance, looking to edge closer to get off good shots. The area was close to the door and had a large glass window next to it.

While standing, smiling, holding expensive bottles of champagne, cigars, and flashing large wads of cash, the hitter felt this to be his best opportunity to take a shot.

PEWN!

He fired the first round. Chaos ensued, with the crowd scattering every-which-way, trying to avoid being a casualty of the situation.

PEWN!

Another shot rang. The large light above was knocked out, leaving the place sparsely lit.

PEWN! PEWN! PEWN! PEWN! PEWN!

Five additional shots were let off. Three people were hit before the gunman then scrambled after the brazen assault, running amongst the crowd.....

The majority of those taking pictures jump to the occasion to cover and protect Drip. However, he hadn't gotten hit.

Ayonna, Lilly, and Von had, with him suffering the most severe wounds. He was down bad, and bleeding out heavy. Not too long afterwards, Von blacked out…..

Chapter 1

Several Months Prior....

Bill Hilliard and his partner Valente Canelo, often preferring to go by Valco, were provided a crucial piece of surveillance footage of a possible getaway car that was used by the assailant who'd shot Feezy and killed his daughter. There was a camera inside the light post on the corner where the shooting took place, and a tag number on a light gray Ford Taurus was picked up. The car was registered to a Johnny Lee Washington, better known on the streets as "J-Dubb." Bill and Valco were on their way to the home address on file for the car to have a look at it and confirm a match and to also question Mr. Washington if possible. He lived with his mother.

"Very good thinking on your behalf, Valco, to check the camera from the light posts in the area. And the way that car fled the scene after the fact, it *had* to be the shooter inside," Bill said to his esteemed colleague and partner.

"Homeland security did bless us on that, didn't they? Thanks to them, we now have more than two thousand security cameras all over the City of Philadelphia," responded Valco.

"Yes we do, Yes...We do. Now all that's left is to verify the car and have a look at the owner. We definitely have a match. And also, the nine-one-one call made by Richardson himself took place eighteen seconds after the car was spotted on footage. We have an eyewitness too."

"The elderly lady, Miss Ethredge, right?"

"Absolutely. She had mentioned hearing multiple gunshots then immediately looking out her living room window, and seeing a *gray or white egg shaped car hauling-ass to get away,*' in her own words," said Bill.

"And a late nineties model Ford Taurus is shaped like an egg," responded Valco.

"Exactly. I had one of those cars. A ninety-seven model. So we have too many variables at our disposal, to not be correct."

"Confirmation and a line of questioning to make Washington have a hiccup on what he's done or may know, and we'll be on the right track," Valco expressed.

Shortly thereafter, the two homicide detectives arrived at the home of J-Dubb's mother, Mrs. Carolyn Washington. Getting out the car and walking up to the door, Bill then knocked.

After taking a look out the front window, Mrs. Carolyn noticed the unmarked department car parked before her home and answered.

"Who is it?"

"Philadelphia Police, Ma'am. May we have a word with you please?" stated Bill.

The old lady slowly opened the door. She was separated from the two officers by burglar bars.

"May I help you?" Mrs. Carloyn asked.

"Yes, how are you? I'm Detective Bill Hilliard, and this is my colleague, Valente Canelo. We're here to see Johnny Lee Washington. Would he be a resident here?"

"Yes. This is my son's residence. Might I ask, in God's name, what has that boy done now, sir?" Mrs. Carolyn asked, anxiety was beginning to set in.

"Well, ma'am, to speak the truth, your son hasn't done *anything* to our knowledge. We want to question him about his whereabouts a few weeks back. His car was caught on a city camera, fleeing the scene of a shooting. We got the license plate number. This address was on file," Bill explained.

"Oh Lord! The boy keeps my blood pressure high and my nerves on edge. He just refuses to leave them drugs alone. He's not here at the moment, officer. You may wanna try back about five or six."

"Ma'am, can you tell us what kinda car your son owns?" Valco asked.

"Actually, I brought the car and let him do all the driving on it. It's a Ford Taurus, a nineteen ninety-eight model," she confirmed.

Bill and Valco looked at one another. Valco pulled a small notepad from his pocket and jotted down notes. They'd provided Mrs. Carolyn with a photo of a light gray Taurus that was printed from the internet.

"Is the car your son drives like this?" Bill questioned.

"Yes, it is. Same color and type. But why would my son be involved a getaway from a shooting?" Mrs. Carolyn asked.

"Ma'am, I can't speak on that at the moment until I speak with your son first. Is it any way I can get you to assure me that you'll hold him in place here and give us a call when he's home?" Bill held out his card to offer her.

She looked him in the eyes strongly, in the sense more so of begging for help, than being concerned of her son possibly being in trouble. She then reached through the bars with her fingers to retrieve the card.

"Please give us a call when your son is home, ma'am. We'd like to get down to the bottom of this and clear him of any blame. That's all we're aiming to do. And we never got your name, ma'am?" Bill stated.

"It's Carolyn…Carolyn Washington," she responded.

Bill then extended his hand to shake hers. Valco did the same.

"Have a nice day, Miss Carolyn. You take care now, okay." Bill lastly said.

"You two as well."

The two policemen got back into the car, fired it up, and pulled away.

$$\$\$\$\$\$$$

Several Hours later...

Keeping her word to Bill, Mrs. Carolyn called him like she said she would, to have a brief talk.. However, her son–J Dubb–had done like he normally did. He didn't come home. And more than likely, he wouldn't be for the next couple days or more.

"Bill Hilliard here," he answered.

"Hello, Mister Hilliard. Carolyn Washington here."

"Hey! I'm glad you called. Your son finally made it home?"

"No sir. He has not. I don't know if he will or not. I gave you my word I'd give you a call. You **specifically** *said when my son got home to do so. But I got worried and now I'm ready to get down to the bottom of things."*

"Any idea when he will return?"

"I can't say. He often goes days or even weeks without doing so. And I know you're ready to ask him the questions you have, to find out what you need to know."

"I am, ma'am. And we will. Just please have him to know that we'd like to speak with him," Bill said.

"Would it help if I gave you his cell phone number?"

Bill was handed a gem from her with those words. Not only would he be able to track J-Dubb's movement and phone calls from that night but afterwards too, following the shooting. Now, they would know who he'd been in contact with and track them too. More dots on the page and a consistent pattern to trail behind, made it far better to connect the dots and draw a promising picture than it was to not have any. Bill totally understood the benefit of that.

"Why yes, it'll help to provide me with his cell phone number. That'll help in a major way...."

Bill expressed and excited to know he was about to be provided a treasure trove of material through their person of interest's phone number.

What Bill had in mind to do was have the patrol division issue a BOLO for the Ford Taurus J-Dubb drove, execute a traffic stop on him, then bring him in for questioning to see what he had to say. By the time he and Valco would have J-Dubb sitting cross from them, they'd have completed tracking everyone that J-Dubb called and texted. They would pay attention to the most frequent numbers in his call log and message history, especially the text messages, since they'd be able to retrieve the actual conversation exchange in their own words. J-Dubb's mother blurted out that her son had a drug problem but didn't say what he craved. Once Bill and his partner become aware of this knowledge, a determination could be made on how J-Dubb's habit related to Feezy and the shooting. The two detectives needed to do a follow up with Feezy anyway about his daughter's death.

$$$$$

A Few Days Later...

Bill and Valco knew that they could find Feezy without having to hunt too much. He was at one of two places, recovering from the wounds he'd suffered. That was at his mother's house or at the home of his daughter's mother. They met Dedra's mother on the night of the killing to deliver the bad news. Of all people, she'd been the one to welcome them back the most. They decided to check Esha's place first.

When they made it to her house, Feezy wasn't there. However, she wanted to talk to them about some of *everything*.

Richardson's criminal activities and drug dealing endeavors perhaps? Bill thought to himself, making a facial expression to Valco.

Bill called her prior to their arrival, wanting to be sure that she was there. Esha stood at the door and welcomed them inside.

"Please tell me y'all done found out who killed my baby, sir?" Esha inquired as a tear rolled down her face.

"Not yet, Miss Davis. We're getting close. We were hoping to meet Stephon over here to find out if he had recalled anything. He wasn't able to in the initial interview," Bill stated.

"Feezy don't stay here full-time. I let him come over every so often because we're both still going through it together about our daughter," responded Esha.

"Where is he now?" asked Bill.

"I don't know. He somewhere out there, doing what he does, and not seeming to want to know who in the hell killed our baby and tried to kill him."

"Miss Davis..." Valco chimed in. "Any idea why this happened? Who wanted Stephon dead?"

"Feezy in them streets heavy. *Something* happened out there!! Ain't no doubt about that. More than likely, he got into it with somebody or a few people. He stayed in some mess. And now, that bastard done had *whoever* come looking to kill him but got my baby in the process."

"What did he tell you had happened? What was it all about?" asked Bill.

"He told me somebody tried to rob him for those shopping bags and my car. A lot of that is going on," Esha revealed.

Feezy had provided Bill and Valco a totally different story than he had the mother of his daughter. Valco made a note of her version, then allowed Bill to proceed with the questions.

"What time you expecting him here today?"

"We don't really have a set time. He just comes by. He just comes and goes how he sees fit. I gave him a key again. And whenever I call him to come, he'll do so ," Esha said.

"Can you call him now? We'll greatly appreciate it if we could speak to both of you together." Valco pleaded, now finding an angle to work her to reveal more.

"And if possible, can we have the new number he has, so we can notify him directly when we find out additional information to get us closer to capturing the person who took your daughter away from you?" stated Bill, playing the empathy role with her to gain her trust.

Esha gave them the new number without a problem. Bill's plan had worked. He had Feezy's number all along, the original one that hadn't changed. He lied to her in the event Feezy had. However, Esha provided a second number as well, being that Feezy had two phones. Valco documented it all.

Searching through her contacts, Esha dialed Feezy's number and he answered, putting him on speaker. That was habit of hers, to talk to each and every person aloud. He was no different.

"Hello!"

"Feezy, I need you to come by the house as soon as you can," Esha said to him.

"What's wrong? Everything okay? He responded, a tone of panic was in his voice by her wording a request the way she had.

"Yeah, everything okay. I got Bill and the other man over here updating me on Dedra's killing," she informed.

"Who?"

Feezy had forgotten the name of the lead detective.

"The guy Bill, from Philly Homicide, Feezy."

"What the fuck! What they want?!"

He remembered now.

14

*"What you mean, **what they want?!** What you **think** they want! They here to talk to you again about Dedra's killing. And you need—-"*

*"Maaann! I told you, Esha....We **done** talking to them! We're gonna let this process take place and take care of itself. You already know what we talked about, so why—"*

"Motherfucka, these people trying to help us with this case! And the last I knew, they doing ten times better jobs than you!" Esha barked at Feezy. *"Your ass ain't did **nothing** to try to get down to the bottom of it! My damn daughter got **killed**, Feezy, while she was out with **you!** Somebody tried to kill you behind some shit you did or got going on! So I **suggest** you get your ass over here to talk to these people or don't come back **ever** again! Go to the other bitch's house, Shayla, you got!"* Esha had a long moment to vent.

Bill and Valco both jarred their heads at the fiery domestic exchange.

"Whatever, Esha! Whatever!" Feezy barked back then disconnected the call on Esha.

"I know this motherfucka didn't just hang up on me!" She let out then hurriedly redialed his number. Bill placed his hand over hers to prevent her from doing so.

The two police veterans knew they could work her more alone than they could if the father of her deceased daughter were there to assist her. And not only that, she was a scorned, mad, black woman, who'd not long gotten done arguing with an ex. In that state of mind, she'd be willing to spill her guts on every illegal thing that she knew Feezy had done and was currently involved with in real time. Knowing this, Bill threw gas on the fire.

"Where does Stephon work?" he asked in a calm way.

Bill already knew Feezy sold drugs for a living.

"That motherfucka don't work no damn where! He's a drug dealer! And somebody done killed my baby behind the street shit he got going on!" she vented. Technically, snitching on dude. On purpose.

"And who is Shayla? The other female you mentioned?" Valco asked. He was aiming to hit on something since they had a name they'd never heard before.

Esha sucked her teeth and rolled her eyes at the thought of Shayla and the utterance of her name. She then went on to relate her dislike of the girl who'd taken her daughter's dad away from her for the time being.

"Shayla Allen is her name. That bitch ain't shit! I can't stand her ass. She and Feezy was together for a little while... until they got into it. He told me things went too far with them one day and she shot at his ass," Esha stated.

"She shot at him?" Bill asked with a bit of shock to his voice.

Valco jarred his head at the same time.

"Yep. That's what he told me," she responded.

Valco immediately wrote down on paper what Esha had said. They definitely had obtained more to work with throughout the interview. The intent from the point was to intensify the investigation, gather more potential evidence, compare notes and cross reference them, then do everything necessary to gain a lead and make an arrest.

The dynamic detective duo were on the job with full force.

Chapter 2

Since the night of Von and Chloe's conversation when he revealed he'd brought the New Year in with another female, she seemed to become vexed on doing something to get back at him in every way possible. Chloe had it in mind to party more on the weekends, live a bohemian lifestyle (a strong and independent female who felt like she didn't need a man), and liberate herself farther through sexual activities with whom she so please. This mind-set was the main reason why she wanted to have an open-relationship with Von to begin with. He agreed and had no problem with what she wanted because he had options. Chino took up a lot of Chloe's time now and Raul had his fair share of it as well.

As for Von, he rarely stayed at the house that he and Chloe shared together. Truthfully, he was all over the place, from one location to the next, which was more suitable for him and how he now lived than before. Von had money and product at each place he laid his head and was moving up the food chain, feeling invisible and unstoppable.

Him and Monyetta were returning to her place one night from a Philadelphia 76ers game when he'd gotten a call from a number he didn't recognize. Curiosity compelled him to answer, as he normally wouldn't do so any other time.

"Yeah! Who is this?" Von asked.

"What's good, playboy. How you be?" the male's voice on the other end responded.

"I'm smooth. But who is this?" Von still didn't recognize the voice.

"Vonnie! Your dad, son," Little Hound revealed.

"Oh shit! What up, Pop! How you doing, my G!" Von was excited as ever to hear his father's voice. They haven't talked since the days of his visits.

"I been good, son. Just maintaining the struggle, that be all. What you up to?"

"Just cooling. In a new whip I bought not too long ago. I just left a Sixers game, me and a tight little piece of work I got in my life now. We were courtside, Pop," Von said to his dad, looking to impress him and seeking to gain grace and approval of his father.

"That's what's up there, son. Fam, Drip told me you might be up in the world."

"Oh okay. I was wondering how you got the new number."

"Kiki gave it to me. We've been in constant contact. I got her taking care of something for me. I'll let you know more about it as it plays out," replied his father.

"Check that. You straight though? You need something? I wanna bless you with a couple dollars. I'm up now, Pop," Von informed.

"What's understood doesn't need to be explained, son. Especially not over the phone. You know what I mean," Little Hound cautioned about talking loosely on the phone, if at any time for that matter.

"I get your point, Pop. And you're right. But how much can you use? And where do I need to send it?"

"Whatever you got for me, just give it to Kidada. Like I said, I've got her on top of something for me."

"Bet that. But look, how much longer you gotta be in there?"

"Shit, if everything go through like I need it to, it'll be this year or maybe next," his father revealed.

"That's what's up, Pop. That is what's up, you feel me."

BLOODLINE OF A SAVAGE II | PRINCE A. TAUHID

"No doubt. But what type of new whip you got and who's your new sweetheart?"

"Oh, I'm in a Dodge Magnum. Black on black. An o-eight jawn. And my girl's name is Monyetta. You wanna speak to her for a moment?"

"I don't mind. But check. I strongly advise you to start putting the paper away to benefit you in the long run. This recession shit for real, son. You better take heed."

"Ah shit, we gonna be a'ight. I think that smart-ass nigga, Obama, gonna fix everything. And by the way, the recession ain't stopped Jerry Jones from spending a billion bucks or more on a new football stadium for them Dallas 'Cowgirls' to play in. But my Eagles gonna continue to fly high over them no matter what," Von stated, joking with his pop.

"Boy, you hell! Ha Ha Ha! I like that one. **Fly Eagles Fly!** *And yeah, let me speak with your shorty for a moment... since you speak so highly about her,"* responded his father.

Little Hound continued to entertain and talk on the phone with his son and the girlfriend for a time longer until they concluded the call.

Moments later before Von reached Monyetta's apartment, he'd gotten another call. It was Rosa. Her voice sounded down about something. Distraught in a way. She wanted to see him. And not tomorrow. But rather right away. Von let her know he'd be by shortly.

He and Monyetta arrived at her place and the two walked inside. Von took a seat on the couch because he had no intent to stay long. Monyetta made her way to her bedroom to get into something more comfortable to sleep in.

"You staying with me tonight?" she asked upon returning to her living room.

"It's a good possibility. I gotta take care of some business first though. You gonna be up tonight?"

"Now Von, you know I take my education very seriously. I've got classes tomorrow. And by the way, I'm looking to switch majors."

"Oh you are. To what now?"

"Journalism. I wouldn't mind aspiring to be a news anchor for one of the hometown stations. Also, my interest has peaked in a way to be a writer. Being a journalist first would make that process easier for me as a novelist or a screenwriter," Monyetta expressed.

"Sound like you know what you wanna do with your life, sweetheart. That's a good thing," Von responded, then stood to his feet and readied himself to leave.

The two hugged and kissed.

"Thank you for showing me a good time tonight, Von. You're my type of guy."

"You're welcome, babe. Anytime, boo. We have so much more in stow in our future. It's very bright. So bright to where, when you get out of class tomorrow, we going shopping for shades and for some accessories, baby. How does that sound?"

"Sounds sweet to me. But what would sound more sweeter is if I can come home from school tomorrow, take a shower, and have you ask me, 'are you ready to get out and do some shopping like we want to?'," Monyetta stated, then withdrew a keychain from inside her pajama top with an extra key to her place on the end of it.

She smiled as she offered it to Von. He returned an even brighter one as he accepted.

"So this what we doing now? This what you want?" he asked.

"I speak with my actions, Trevon. And, we doing whatever you want to do," the chocolate cutie responded, then kissed him slowly. "I'm following your lead. A strong young black female behind a strong young black man," she said then kissed him once more.

"Now go ahead and handle your business, sweetheart. I'll be here when you get back," Monyetta assured him then turned and made her way to the bedroom to rest up.

Von's cell phone vibrated yet again. Rosa was calling. He exited the apartment and answered while going down the steps.

"I'm on my way now, okay," he said upon answering.

"Please get here, Von. Something's not right," Rosa responded in a tone that let Von know she was crying and in an emotional state of being.

He knew exactly what that was all about. Her brother being missing and not picking up his phone. Von had a sympathetic role to play now, and would do so to the fullest, since he was the killer and knew what had happened to Alfredo. He'd been murked and put down forever. Dude wasn't ever coming back.

$$$$$

Kidada Savage, the daughter of Hound Jr and sister of Von, made her way to downtown Center City, Philadelphia, to the law offices of Klein & Jacobson Attorneys At Law. She had an appointment to specifically meet with the son of the highly esteemed and legally astute, Byron Jacobson and Levi Jacobson. The father retired from the practice and left his eldest of three sons in charge. Jack Klein was the son of Frank Klein, a senior litigator and bosom buddy of Byron's, replacing his father at the office as well.

Kidada had in her possession portions of her father's case file and an omnibus of legal motions Little Hound wanted his new attorney to review for substance and merit, to determine if they were adoptable or not. The motions had been researched and typed by a "Jailhouse Lawyer" there at Coleman with Hound Jr. and the paralegal inmate knew his work.

The young Savage melanated beauty was properly dressed as her father instructed her to be. She looked like business and money and displayed the manners and mindset to go along with the persona she gave up.

The five-foot six inch hundred thirty pound daddy's girl entered the building and took the elevator to the office suite. Kidada had on a nice pair of shades, an expensive scarf, and a designer labeled coat the scarf matches. She approached the desk of the receptionist to make her aware of who she was there to see.

"Hello, ma'am! Welcome to Klein and Jacobson Attorneys At Law. How may we serve you?" the tall, skinny, pale female greeted. She had powder blue eyes and blonde hair pinned in a bun.

Kidada looked in her hand at the note she had. "Yes ma'am, I'm here to see a Mister Levi Jacobson," she responded.

"And you are?"

"I'm Miss Kidada Savage. I have a ten o'clock appointment."

The receptionist keyed in the information. Most likely the last name.

"There you are. I'll notify him that you're here, ma'am. If you will, please have a seat and Mister Jacobson shall be with you shortly, okay," the apparently Jewish female related to Kidada.

"Yes ma'am."

Kidada took a space on the plush leather couch and began to thumb through one of the interesting looking magazines that sat atop the glossy coffee table in front of her. There was one other person in the lobby waiting to be seen along with Kidada. An elder white male.

Prior to the receptionist locating Kidada's name on the appointment list, she'd looked on at the well-dressed black female as if she was one out of place. Like she'd gotten off on the wrong floor or something to that effect. Kidada recognized the suspicious glance shot at her. She returned one with a bigger caliber of an invincible bullet of shade. Nearly thirty minutes later, Kidada noticed that Mr. Jacobson was finally ready to see her.

The lovely daughter of Hound Savage II stood to her feet and sauntered towards the direction led by the legal assistant who appeared from the back. Nearly forty-five steps later down the hallway, Kidada stood face-to-face with the man who held the legal talent and skill to possessing persuade a federal judge to free her father.

Levi Jacobson was a six foot two, one hundred sixty pound scrawny guy, who had a clean-shaven head and face. He had on a silver suit, a metallic purple silk tie, and a pair of black leather shoes with wing tips.

"Miss Savage?" Levi asked.

"I am. Mister Levi Jacobson?" Kidada replied.

"Yes...That'll be me. Come inside please. Welcome to my office."

"I'm glad to be here. On behalf of my father," she remarked with a smile, entering the office then taking a seat in one of the large brown leather chairs in front of Levi's desk.

He took his place back at his workstation, keying in a thread of information on his computer to draw up his client's profile, then the discussion between him and Kidada began.

"Mister Jacobson, I have this package of documents my father told me to hand to you, sir," she said, then handed the attorney the thick legal envelopes.

Before that, Levi and Little Hound held extensive conversations over the phone. An attorney-client visit was on schedule for Levi. He would travel to Florida to visit with Kidada's father, as certain aspects of his professional and ethical duties prevented Levi from speaking with the daughter about. It had to be discussed by the lawyer directly with the client.

Kidada's meeting lasted about an hour with the lawyer. Levi imparted as much of the case with her as he was able to do. The client had a lot going good for him in regard to the errors and technicalities. The main issue that stood out for Levi to use was to file a claim of ineffective assistance against Little Hound's trial lawyer, amongst other things. Kidada was provided with a great sense of hope from the visit. She was ready to have her father back out in free society with her and their family.

Chapter 3

Bill and his brilliant investigative side-kick, Valco, were called upon to report to the landfill by the Crime Scene Unit. One of the local trash trucks had dumped its contents, and a body was discovered amongst the pile of garbage held in a mound. Apparently, a human leg had broken through the triple layered trash bags the body had been stuffed in, and one of the sanitation workers took notice then alerted his supervisor. The Nike sneakers and jean pants were still on the victim. The first policemen to arrive used a pocket knife to cut open the bags to be sure that it was indeed a human body inside. It was. The trash truck that contained the body patrolled the North Philly neighborhood, Bill and Valco's jurisdiction, so the investigation belonged to them.

The two were there to find out what new case they had on their hands.

"What we have here, Gavin?" Bill asked of the police veteran already present on the scene.

"A Latino looking, probably early twenties, most likely street dwelling male here, judging by all the tattoos he's got all over his arms and neck," informed Gavin Lowe, a fifteen year officer on the force.

Bill and Valco then began to put on rubber examination gloves and approached the body. They prodded the pockets of the clothes the victim had on and ran their hands over and reached for any objects that may have been in his pockets. There was nothing inside. They then took a look at the body to determine what may was the cause of death. No doubt, a homicide had to have occurred for a person to be stuffed in a triplet of trash bags and thrown out. Now all left to find was… how did the guy die?

The body was pulled from the pile and laid out to be placed into a body bag. Upon lifting the body from the garbage, blood poured forth from the back of the head. A long thick noodle string of brain plopped out and dangled as well.

"Oh God!" Bill grimaced and exclaimed at the sight of the oozing decomposing organ, gagging a bit behind the smell of the garbage and a dead body.

"What the hell?!" Valco let out.

He couldn't hold it in any longer. Valco threw up then and there on the spot. His stomach wasn't as strong as Bill's.

Bill leaned over to have a look.

"We got a bullet hole there," he pointed then took a look at the face of the victim.

"No exit wound in the face. And that's a large hole in the back of the head," Bill remarked to the others and then partly opened his mouth to have a look.

"Teeth missing in the front. Whoever this guy ran afoul with, had to be really pissed off to ram the barrel of a high caliber pistol into his mouth and pull the trigger. We got a hole through the mouth that goes straight to the brain and out the back," Bill made them aware.

Valco looked on and took notes of all he observed and of what Bill stated.

Bill looked at the Sanitation Supervisor and spoke to him.

"If you don't mind, sir, I need the route that the truck had taken from the past four days. I think this guy has been dead for about that long. We're gonna get him down to the crime lab and find out who he is; contact the family to have them make a positive ID; then proceed with the process of investigating his murder. Somebody definitely killed him," confirmed Bill.

He and Valco then took off the gloves that they had on, threw them onto the pile, sanitized their hands, and then left the scene headed to the office. CSI would gather the body from there and do all it was they do. Another day, another body, and another murder for the two added to their list of other homicides that had to be investigated. They had all the time in the world. There was no statute of limitations on murder.

$$\$\$\$\$\$$$

Meanwhile… Four Days Prior….

Von arrived at Rosa's apartments that night to know what the urgency was to have him come over. When he'd gotten there, she related what she wanted. Rosa had tears in her eyes and was so more emotional than Von had ever seen her before.

"What's the problem, Rosa?" he asked upon being let inside.

"Something going on with my brother, Von. His car is out front, but I don't know where he's at and can't get in touch with him. He's not answering his phone, Von. I am very concerned about my brother. This is not like him, bro," Rosa expressed.

Von looked at her to think of what he could say. He had nothing off the top of his head. So he asked what was logical.

"You called Tito to ask him has he seen him or has he been there at the shop?" Von responded.

"Yeah, I did. Tito said he hadn't seen him since New Year's Day. I called my mother and went by her house. She hasn't seen nor heard anything either. My brother bought that car not too long ago, and if it's in the parking lot, that indicates to me that when you dropped me off, that he was in here. He wasn't. So I waited and waited. He never came over. Didn't come get his car. And didn't call," Rosa stated.

Von shook his head, displaying a show of concern and sympathy, before giving Rosa a hug and brainstorming on what to say next.

"I wish I knew what to tell you, Rosa, but I don't. I'm here with you though. And I'm here for you, okay?" he expressed then kissed her on the forehead and smelled her hair.

"I need you to stay here with me tonight, Von. I'm not gonna be able to relax or calm my nerves until I hear from my brother or until he shows up. If Alfredo don't contact someone in the next two days, we're gonna call the cops and make a report."

Von simply looked on at her and didn't say a word. He thought over the last request she'd made. Ain't no way he could tell her he'd be staying. So he had to tell a lie and get back to Monyetta before it got too late. Besides, he didn't want to be around the negative energy Rosa was afflicted with.

"I can't stay tonight, Rosa. I've gotta stay by my grandmother's side. Nana hasn't been feeling too well," he told her.

Von's story was part true and part untrue. Mrs. Edna had a cold that she'd been treating.

"But I can make it my business to swing by in the morning, okay?" he said while maintaining strong eye contact with her.

"You promise? I need you for support, Von, if something is going on with my brother."

*Oh yeah…Something **definitely** going on with that nigga! He's **dead!** And ain't **never** coming back!* Von thought to himself.

"I promise, Rosa. I'll be by in the morning, sweetheart, my word. Okay."

"Okay."

"But in the meantime, continue to call around and try to get in contact with Alfredo. I know he's your only sibling and means the world to you," Von said.

"He definitely does," Rosa responded.

The two then kissed and Von left, got into his car, and went to check on his grandmother. Going forward, he would keep one of his pistols tucked in his waistband, in the event that any static generated that would implicate him or his homies. The longer Alfredo remained missing, the more reason for those in his circle could believe the truth of what they'd done had come back to haunt him, and maybe them to. Von and his crew had to remain locked and loaded.

Chapter 4

Presently....

Since taking over the particular territory in West Philly, by knocking off Tyrell and Anton, Ron, Lonnie, and Kareem needed additional hustlers to sell bundles of the heroin product they had. No group of dealers fit the need that they wanted like Shayla and Tangee did. Cori left the motel where they'd been staying and went back to her place. Her hairstyling skills and business forced her to return, as her clients wouldn't stop calling, and she was halfway ready to get back to what she did anyway.

Ron contacted Cold Heart and let him know that the two females on the team could come on that side of town to bang their packs until the nigga, Feezy, was finally tracked down and his threat eliminated forever. Cold Heart agreed and went to get Shayla and Tangee, so they could do their thing, then return to the motel once the work day came to an end. The two girls were still in contact with J-Dubb too as he was their main man to call upon for transportation with his car, the Ford Taurus he owned.

J-Dubb had been told by his mother that two policemen came by the house looking for him and that they wanted to question him about something. Mrs. Carolyn had left out the part where she'd been specifically told by Bill and Valco that the car he drove was captured on camera fleeing a shooting. J-Dubb barely went home from that day and thought maybe he was wanted for any number of minor offenses committed on his behalf.

One day, J-Dubb had not long dropped off Shayla and Tangee at the new location on the West Side. He was back in North Philly, headed to where a small crowd of other dope shooters gathered to do their thing in the a.m. He had sixty dollars' worth of it that Shayla had given him. J-Dubb was ready to get high.

WHOOP-WHOOP-WHOOP-WHOOP!

J-Dubb's mind was so preoccupied on the product he had in his pocket and the high he was craving, that he'd paid no attention to the cop car that had been following him for the past ten blocks he'd driven. Back up had been called. And now, there were four cars surrounding the gray Ford. Bill's request for a BOLO and to execute a stop and arrest for questioning were being fulfilled by the traffic stop. After hearing the sirens, J-Dubb pulled over.

The eyewitness, Mrs. Pearl Etheridge, had already confirmed that the car she'd seen fleeing once the gunshots stopped, was indeed the one in the photo Bill showed her. So the correct car was identified, and the tag was called in to confirm the person of interest.

The cop who'd pulled J-Dubb over approached.

"License and registration sir!" The policeman growled out.

"Officer, why was I—"

"License and registration I said! I'm the man who asking all the questions," the cop retorted, becoming more aggressive now.

"You know what... fuck that!" J-Dubb was now getting agitated and frustrated at the situation. He was anxious to pump the powerful heroin he had in his pocket into his vein.

In a rash way, J-Dubb reached over to the glove compartment to get his credentials, grumbling words of insult in the process.

"-----Slowly there!" the cop barks. "And keep your hands where I can see them!" he demanded and the other policemen positioned their hands on their pistols.

J-Dubb tossed his hands in the air in surrender. "A'ight-a'ight, goddamnit! A'ight!" he let out.

He retrieved his wallet then slowly handed it over to the officer.

The cop then flipped open the tattered leather holder and immediately took notice at the name on the driver's license and the other name which appeared on the registration material. He withdrew his pistol and proceeded with the duty he had.

"Johnny Lee Washington! We have an outstanding warrant for your arrest!"

$$\$\$\$\$\$$

Two Hours Later....

J-Dubb was now down at the police station, sitting in the interrogation room, cuffed to the table. He'd been told that a homicide detective issued a warrant to have him brought in for questioning. Throughout the traffic stop and apprehension of J-Dubb, he fucked around and racked up a new charge. A possession of heroin offense behind those three $20 baggies he had in his pocket that Shayla given him.

J-Dubb felt like he had nothing to fear and thought he was going through yet another routine traffic stop like so many times before, leaving his mother with the burden of paying the citation as she always had. But not this time. The stakes were higher. Something far more serious had occurred. A murder that was. And the car he drove was at the center of it all.

Bill and Valco entered the room and found J-Dubb half asleep with his head on the table. He'd rose from his slumber upon hearing the door closing behind Valco.

"Well-Well-Well... *Johnny Lee Washington.* The grown man who still gives his poor mother problems just like a little boy would," spat Bill.

"The fuck you talking 'bout!" And why the fuck am I here?!" J-Dubb barked in retort. He had a nappy mini afro stuffed under a dirty smelly skull cap and a dingy unwashed cloth material jacked on to keep him warm.

Bill sat a file of papers on the table. The day before, he had J-Dubb's phone records pulled up and printed out from the previous three months and made stunning discoveries of a repetitive phone number in his call-log that matched the same in Feezy's call-log for a period of time. The only difference was that the contact between the owner of the repetitive number and Feezy had stopped a few weeks prior to the shooting of Feezy and his daughter. But a few calls from the number to J-Dubb occurred the same day as the shooting. About an hour or so before and thirty minutes after. Who did the number belong to? Bill pondered.

"How you doing, J-Dubb?" Bill stated. He learned the street name from the text messages of the phone records.

"Dude, you don't know me like that. And again, might I ask.....Why- the- fuck- am- I here?" J-Dubb responded.

Although he was a notorious heroin junkie from hell, J-Dubb was a college graduate and smart guy gone bad. An educated fool, so to speak. And had no plan to change course anytime soon on who he was and what he do.

Bill opened the folder he had and began to inform J-Dubb why he was brought in.

"We have you here, Johnny, because your car was picked up on one of our city street cameras, fleeing the scene of a shooting. A father was shot and a little girl killed."

"Man, look, how many goddamn Ford Taurus' you think rolling around Philly?! How the hell *my* car out of all them did you came to the conclusion is *that* car?" J-Dubb stated as he nodded his head to point at the photo of his vehicle in the picture in front of him.

"All these other Ford Taurus' that you mention doesn't have the same tag number that your car does there, now do it?" Bill pointed to another image that clearly showed his license plate.

J-Dubb lowered his head to focus his eyes sharply on what he was looking at. He knew then that the car belonged to him but didn't voice it.

"So where were you on the night of December eighteenth at about seven-thirty? May I ask?" Bill went into the question farther.

"Well, first of all, I ain't have nothing to do with *anybody* being shot and especially nothing to do with a kid dying! I'm a dope fiend, man! Not a killer! I do heroin. I don't do hits!" J-Dubb protested vehemently.

"Do you have any idea who Stephon Richardson is?" Valco asked.

"Who?"

"Stephon Richardson? He goes by the name Feezy," stated Bill.

"Never heard of him. If he's not a heroin junkie I run with or a dealer I buy from…I have no clue who he is," J-Dubb related.

Bill thought of something. It came to him that Feezy had no history of dealing heroin but rather, sold crack cocaine. He then placed a picture of Feezy in front of J-Dubb.

"This guy… You know him?"

J-Dubb took a closer look. Indeed, he had seen Feezy once or twice upon going to cop a fix from Shayla but hardly recalled knowing who he was. He squinted his eyes and strained to remember. There was no immediate knowing who he was.

"Nah, still don't know who dude is."

Valco posed a question or two. "Who do you know lives on Cecil B. Moore? Anybody?"

"I don't hang around Cecil B. Moore, and I don't know anybody who does either," J-Dubb responded.

"Well, who the hell had your car that night? And who the hell is *'Baby girl'* you got as a contact in your phone? It seems like you and her had a lot of communication before the shooting your car was seen fleeing from. And, thirty minutes after that, the same *'Baby Girl'* gives you a call. Why was that so? And not only that…Baby girl's phone number is heavily in the call log of **that guy** right there!" Bill spat and pointed.

"Now I suggest you get to talking right now motherfucka or we about to book your ass on murder one and attempted murder!" Bill added to his rant.

"Look man, I told you, I don't know shit about nobody being shot or about nobody being killed! That's my story and I'm sticking to it! And Baby girl know some of everybody. So it wouldn't surprise me if her number ended up in a lot of motherfucka's call logs. That's her business. Not mine," J-Dubb stressed.

"And I'm done talking to you motherfuckas too! If you wanna book me for those three baggies of dope, be my guest. I ain't gonna do nothin' but get sent to a rehab treatment center for them anyway, so. Do as you may. Fine by me."

Valco came to realize that they had not requested that the frequent phone number in both J-Dubb's and Feezy's call logs be tracked, to know where the person who owned the phone was located that night. The cell tower had to have recorded the pinging from the phone. And if J-Dubb was anywhere in that proximity at the time, they'd know. An additional request would need to be made to know where J-Dubb and essentially *"Baby Girl"* was situated that night. Then, the process could narrow down from that point moving towards.

"Okay, buddy. Not a problem for us. You're *now* being charged with the murder of Dedra Richardson, the little girl who was killed, and the attempted murder of her father, Stephon Richardson, Johnny! In addition to heroin possession!" declared Bill with an angry feeling in his voice.

"This is bullshit! I want a lawyer!" J-Dubb yelled to Bill's and Valco's backs as they walked out the interview room.

Chapter 5

Von and another homie of his that he was really cool with, Jeffery Toliver, were posted up outside a bar located on 8th and Diamond in North Philly. Jeff was also a good friend of Cold Heart as well. The three of them had been tight for a long time. Jeff had become part of the team alongside Von and Cold Heart since he wanted to crossover from selling coke. He'd been offered a position and gladly accepted. Von brought him along for a ride as the two were out looking for territory they could take over and have Jeff making as his own. The area was run by a dude who was considered a bonafide weakling and chump by all Philly street standards. He had no power to keep others in check and was not able to protect what he had. His name was Tobias Flowers, a somewhat short and slim guy who had a career as a boxer, in addition to dope dealing.

The sun had not long set on a Friday evening. Von and Jeff decided to scout out turf, and Tobias was seated in one of his low profile cars he drove, talking with a female he had with him. He was parked at a short distance from the front door of the bar. About eighty feet down the block. Von nor Jeff saw him. But he had his eyes on them. Tobias was trying to figure out what the two was up to? He was somewhat familiar with Von but not so much Jeff. Von was in his Dodge Magnum and was parked along the curb across from the bar, The Blue Flame.

As Von and Jeff stood and observed the people and express street lingo, a brown Chevy Suburban appeared and attempted fitting the full-sized S.U.V. into the awfully tight space between Von's Magnum and another car in front of it. The owner of the Suburban was Kovan Lassiter, a thirty-nine year old guy from the neighborhood.

As Kovan pulled ahead, then backup and pulled up, then back up, he bumped into Von's car and broke the front left headlight.

WHAM!

"Yo nigga! What the fuck you got going on, motherfucka!" Von spat as he approached.

Kovan pulled the Suburban alongside the car in front of the damage Dodge, put on his hazard lights, then got out to see what he'd done.

"What the fuck, nigga?! Look what you did! And your apology not gonna pay for that there, motherfucka! **Money will!** My shit brand new!" Von said vehemently. He stood face to face with the guy as he barked in his face.

"Look, homie… I ain't got money on me like that. But, my truck insured. We can call the cops and have them–"

"Nah-nah-nah, nigga! We ain't doing none of that shit! You wasn't screaming that insurance shit when you crashed into my ride, was you?! And you not about to do it now! So you might as well un-ass that cash and pay me for damaging my shit! I want a rack right now, nigga!" Von cut off the dude's words and demanded.

"Man I told you, I ain't got no money on me like that!" The guy got louder now with Von. He had a little more size than Von and felt disrespected by the harsh and aggressive tone in Von's voice.

"Why you keep coming at me, my nigga, like I'ma bitch or something! Ain't none of that going over here! Now, we can have a cop come make a report, and my insurance company can handle the shit, so we can leave it like it is and that'll be the end of it because I ain't with all the back and forth, my nigga! Like for real!" Kovan blew fire now in retort.

"What's up, nigga?!" Von exclaimed, with a vicious mean-mug on his face as anger and rage were beginning to overtake him.

Jeff looked at Von like he was waiting for him to now react to the perceived form of disrespect Kovan had thrown. If Von wasn't able to properly check a motherfucker who talked shit to him after banging into his car, how could he be able to check anybody else, if need be, once they grabbed the particular piece of turf they were looking to have as their own? The homie Jeff simply stood in his place, jarred his head, and produced a concerning look on his face.

Von didn't waste any more of his time tongue wrestling with the dude. He snatched his pistol from his waistline, raised it head level on Kovan, and pulled the trigger.

POW!

He shot the guy point blank then and there. Kovan was dead before he hit the pavement. Blood leaked from the hole he now had in his head.

"What the fuck?!" Tobias was taken aback and in a state of shock at what he saw.

He cranked his car, put it in gear, and got the hell on about his business, him and the female he had with him. The BMW Tobias drove sped away in a hurry.

Von and Jeff got into his car and fled the scene themselves. He now had another body under his belt that he may or may not have to deal with at some point later down the line.

Someone driving by spotted Kovan laid out on the street with blood pouring from his head and they called the 911 Emergency Center. The paramedic and the cops would arrive very soon. Now all Von had to worry about was, did anyone see the shooting? And if so, who? Soon, he'd know the truth in the aftermath of his irrational actions. Problems now began to mount for the young promising and smart Savage, grandson of the legendary Hound. Von took that street shit a little too far. And the crazy part about that was, he didn't have to. Nonetheless, he did. So, it is what it is...

Von drove to the place he and Chloe had together. He pulled the banged up Dodge Magnum into the garage and let down the door to it. He and Jeff then put the cover on it and went upstairs into the apartment. Chloe was home. She was shocked to know Von had brought someone else into their living space. That gave her a strong feeling that something wasn't right. But Von had a normal look on his face and didn't appear to be in an erratic mood to anything that may have happened.

"Hey, baby," Chloe greeted. She was in the kitchen and stepped into the living room upon hearing Von opening the door to their place, jarring her head at the sight of Jeff talking to him.

"I wasn't expecting you home so soon. How was your day?" she checked.

After approaching her, the two then kissed.

"I'm good, sweetie. Had to come home for a moment. This my homie, Jeff, here," Von responded and introduced the friend.

"Hey, Jeff," Chloe said to him, then hurried down the hallway to the bedroom because she had on a small pair of booty-shorts, and Von didn't want her in the presence of his company dressed that way. Not anywhere.

On the way from the shooting scene, he'd called Cold Heart and told him to hurry and get there. It was *urgent*.

Twenty minutes later, the security chief of security was there. Von had already gotten rid of the gun on the way home. He'd thrown it into a water drain, not to be known of for a long time to come.

Cold Heart entered the house. "What the fuck, bro?! What happened?" He knew by the look on Von's face that it was a serious situation.

The three then went down the stairs to the garage for Cold Heart to have a look at the car.

"There was this nut-ass nigga, trying to park a big truck he had into a small space and banged my shit, Cold. Then the nigga hop out, talking all reckless and crazy to me, like I'm a chump! And *he* crashed into **my shit**! So I popped him! Right there on site!" Von stated.

"Where?" Cold Heart wanted to know.

"I domed called that nigga!"

"What! Noo, Von!"

"I had too, Cold. The nigga had a little size to him and got all *brolic* on me, bro. So I had to put him down," Von explained.

"That nigga came for Von, Cold. The way he was shouting about not paying bro, and flexing on him and shit, I was about to blast that bitch-ass nigga myself!" chimed in Jeff.

"What you do with the hammer?" Cold Heart asked.

"That shit gone, bro. I dropped it in a drain," Von made him aware.

"A'ight cool. Hopefully, nobody seen anything. Where it happened at?" Cold Heart asked.

Von gave him the location of where the bar was.

"I'm about to head over there and see what it looks like with the cops. I'll hit you up a little later to let you know what's going on. In the meantime, keep low and don't move the car," Cold Heart stated.

"No doubt, bro," Von responded. He then dapped the both of them.

Cold Heart and Jeff left from the garage, got in his car, and made their way to the scene of the crime.

Von went back up the stairs, prepared to take shower, and was intent on watching the news to find out as much as he could about the dude he'd shot. He knew there wasn't a doubt, that nigga was dead! But the news had a way of exposing information on what the cops had ahead of time.

Von had no intent of telling Chloe anything. Not even about his car being damaged. He wanted to make sure everything was quiet as kept. The less said, the best. He now had a lot going on to concern himself with.

Chapter 6

Three Days Later...

The police had been contacted by an eyewitness of the shooting death of Kovan Lassiter. The witness reported everything that they saw—the fender-bender, the angry exchange of words between the two dudes involved, the one fatal gunshot let off, *everything*—down to the details of it all. The female caller provided the type of car the shooter drove. The cops now were on the lookout for a new model black Dodge Magnum with a broken headlight on the front left corner of the car. The glass fragments that was gathered were in large chucks. Enough in size to know the type of vehicle it belong.

The female witness made it her business to contact law enforcement because she had reason to believe that hers and her boyfriend's lives were in danger from the killer, being that the charcoal gray BMW 5-series was owned by her boyfriend, Tobias Flowers, was spotted by the man who had pulled the trigger. Also, Tobias knew the shooter was a guy he known only as "Von" and feared Von knew who owned the BMW that sped off at the point when the body hit the asphalt. Tobias was the one who pushed his girlfriend, Ella, to call and immediately relate all she'd seen. Something she wanted to do anyway. The cops requested that they come into the station and to provide statements. They were willing to do so. The police entered a BOLO into the system for every black colored Dodge Magnum in the city and who owned them, giving them something to work with.

Von made it his business to go out and get a rental to move about town until his car was repaired. A bit of worry was plaguing him about the overall situation but he had no overall guilty conscience behind taking the guy's life. As with the first killing he'd done of Alfredo, Von professed yet again, "it felt natural to him," and he'd do it again and again, if it got to that point, holding an unusual mind-set and position for a seventeen year old to have. Two people were dead at his hands before he was even an adult, was a lot of reality to take in, as he'd never fathom his life would go in the direction it had; and it was going months before his big day of graduating high school, then go off to college as he had planned to do. The probability of it all was very unlikely at that point. Loom and doom were in the forecast for Von. But honestly, dude didn't give a flying fuck.

$$\$\$\$\$\$$

It was early in the day, around 2:30 p.m., on a Wednesday. Rosa contacted Von and asked him to please come by her house. It was an emergency and she wanted to talk right away, so he went by to see what she wanted. It wasn't good. Rosa was in tears and crying her eyes out.

Arriving at her apartment, she let him in.

"Von! My brother is **dead**! Somebody *killed* him!" Rosa let out hysterically. "I'd been trying to call you all day yesterday and all night… me and my mother had to go and identify his body."

Von began trying to calm her down and console her to the best of his ability since she was very emotional.

"Calm down, baby, calm down. You're gonna have to take it easy, Rosa. Okay. Please," he said to her.

Von hugged her tightly and allowed her to let go of the teary emotions she were experiencing. She sobbed and cried until she'd gotten much as she could out in the moment. The two then took a seat on the couch, and he continued to hold her and plant tender kisses on her forehead.

"You got anywhere to go today? If not, I want you here with me for as long as you can stay. But if you've got things to do, is there any way you can stay here with me later?" Rosa asked.

Von thought over what he had lined up for the day. He wasn't able to hangout or be too loose in the streets like that, due to not fully knowing what was going on in the investigation of the case regarding the guy he'd killed. And until he was one hundred percent in the clear of everything, he would do as Cold Heart suggested and keep low and out the way. That was the best thing he could do. It was cold out anyway as the weather in Philly was most brutal during the last eleven days of January. Plus, the flu was going around badly. And he didn't want the illness or be down bad, but he would go by Monyetta's later, he thought to himself.

"Nah, I ain't got too much to do at the moment. But I can't stay all night though. I'll stay until about nine or ten. Okay?" Von stated to her.

"Anytime of course… yes, right now is better than none. You're here when I need you to be. I can't ask for more," Rosa responded. The two then made their way to the bedroom to lay back and relax. She needed to get her mind off the murder of her brother. Intimacy would help.

Rosa had no knowledge whatsoever that the guy she was laid back with, was the one who'd terminated her brother execution style.

Von could now declare that he was a cold-blooded killer. He was icey! And held no remorse or any feelings. Cold as could be.

Chapter 7

Cold Heart had a serious situation on his hand to work out and put it to rest forever. The necessity to put down the threatening problem weighed heavily on him, more so than it had the member of the crew it concerned most. If he didn't deal with the issue in an immediate type of way, it could harm him and the others to a deep degree. And he was looking to continue to go up the ladder, not down hard in a free fall back to the bottom. He went to Drip and Body about it. They already had somewhat knowledge about it and decided to have another person do all he could to assist with the matter. Enter Pervis, now to resolve the trouble.

Cold Heart contacted the two ladies of the crew—Shayla and Tangee—and made them aware that he was on the way to the motel where they were because he needed to see them about something, Shayla specifically. He and Von had been together that day and went their separate ways about thirty minutes prior upon Cold Heart being contacted and made aware he had a certain type of *package* tightly wrapped in place. A late Christmas gift, so to speak. One that was sure to please for a long time to come.

Von went to see Shayla's sister, Cori. She'd run out of product and needed more. Her spot had begun to do well again, no threats from the cops, or from Feezy for that matter, had occurred, and plenty of money was flowing through to be made.

Between the three of them–Cori, Shayla, and Tangee–they had enough money of their own to buy a really decent car. Being that they needed one, and J-Dubb had not been seen or heard from in weeks, as they often had his car to get around the city in, from the hotel in Jersey across the bridge, back to Philly again to the west area of town, to get money in the new location Ron, Lonnie, and Kareen had control over. The girls were making progress.

Cold Heart pulled up in the parking lot of the motel. He was met by Shayla, standing at the door. She walked to the car, got in, and they rode off.

"I've got a huge surprise for you, Shay… a huge surprise, baby-boo," Cold Heart declared.

"Oh, you do? I get the opportunity to dress for the occasion or what?" She responded.

Cold Heart took a look at her from head to feet with a smile on his face. "Nah. You're good to go as you are. You're gonna like it too. You can thank me later. This may be the best surprise gift you have had in a long time. Probably in your life," Cold Heart excited her with these words as he steered the Firebird.

Shayla returned a really bright smile of her own. A surprise gift was something she needed most to help lift her spirit and make her feel special again, much like she had before being cut. She pulled down the sun visor to observe herself in the mirror and applied a coat of lip gloss. Before exiting the motel, she'd thoroughly brushed her teeth and aptly put on a layer of make-up and eyeliner. Although Shayla had a terribly ugly scar on her face, she still had the duty to maintain all the beauty possessed both inside and out. She closed her purse and smiled.

The time was nearing eight p.m. and the sun had set with and the night was upon them. They'd reached their destination. It was to a mechanic shop and auto body repair. The place was located in West Chester, Pennsylvania, just on the outside of Philly.

Cold Heart drove his car to the back of the place into the garage area. He'd been there before with Body. He and another guy stood at the back of some other car that was parked inside. Shayla was confused like hell at all that was going on.

What the fuck kind of surprise is this?! She'd thought to herself. She still maintained her smile though. "Come on. Time to show you what the surprise is," Cold Heart said as he killed the engine on the car. The doors of the garage then came down.

He and Shayla got out and the two approached Body and the other guy. He was another hitter of Drip's. A dude by the name, Tyler Dunbar, aka "Animal," a former military buddy and close friend of Body.

"This her right here, bro," Cold Heart said. "Shay, met Body and friend... Body, this is Shay."

"Nice to meet you, Shay. I'm so happy to know we were able to help you out and deliver a special gift here for you," Body said to her, extending his hand to shake hers.

"Nice to meet you as well, sir. And Cold has been saying so much about this dog-gone surprise I have in stow, I literally can't wait to see it. Please come on with it. I'm so ready to know what it is," she responded.

Cold Heart, Body, and Animal, all smiled and were impressed at her words,

"I'm a ladies man, Shay. And I love to please. So, it's my pleasure to present your special gift we got for you," Body let out, still maintaining his smile. He then opened the trunk to the 1999 Cadillac Sedan Deville to reveal what was inside.

There he was, that nigga, Feezy, tied tightly at the feet and wrists, with his arms behind his back and a gag around his mouth. His eyes were bucked and he was petrified like no other.

"Motherfucka, you!" exclaimed Shay. "We got your ass now, you bitch ass nigga! Done had some hoe cut my face! It's payback now, pussy!"

A tear rolled from her eye due to emotion.

"Look at me, Feezy! Look at what you done!" she further barked. He squirmed and mumbled with all he had, attempting to plead for mercy.

"What do I get to do to his ass?" Shay looked up at Body and Cold Heart and asked, going back and forth between them both with her eyes.

Body presented an object wrapped in a thick towel. It was a gun, he peeled back the ends to expose.

"Here…" said Body. "It's already ready to shoot."

Shayla took the weapon without any hesitation, reached over into the trunk, put the barrel to the head of a now vehemently squirming Feezy, forcing Body and Animal to hold him steady, and pulled the trigger.

BANG!

"Again!" demanded Cold Heart.

BANG!

"One more time."

BANG!

"Good," Cold Heart concluded.

The problems and threats of Feezy were no more.

They took his body from the car, stuffed him in an oil barrel, poured concrete mix atop him, loaded the barrel on a truck, and prepared to haul it out and be dumped into the river, a lake, or a pond.

Shayla had done a good job. She was proud of her work. Life would be a little easier for her now. She was good to go. Or so it was thought.

$$$$$

Rosa and her Dominquez family made funeral arrangements to bury her brother. Everything had been paid for by the top man of their Puerto Rican loved ones, Tito himself, and the day was at hand to lay Alfredo to rest. The service was to be held at the family's church in North Philly, then, he would be taken to Ivy Hill Cemetery to be buried. Chloe and Von were set to appear and pay their respects to her cousin, as expected of them.

Prior to the day, the investigators contacted Rosa and her mother and requested to come by the place of residence Alfredo was known to have lived. Being he stayed at his sister's place more so than he had at their mother's, the focus of the police was placed heavily on Rosa's, as the authorities wanted to get their hands on important personal effects once owned by Alfredo before his demise–any cell phones, tablet, laptops, legal documents, etc. The material was necessary to aid in the investigation.

Bill Hillard and Valente Canelo had jurisdiction and the duty to handle the case. It was the both of them, who made a stop at the mother's house first, to express condolences and assure her that they'd do all within their power to find out who killed her son and put them away forever if the death penalty isn't sought first.

The duo then went to Rosa's apartment. She led the way, with her mother in the passenger seat, and the investigators trailing behind. Rosa gave them permission to take all they wanted from the place that belonged to Alfredo. There were cellphones retrieved, one tablet, one laptop, and a log journal that Alfredo wrote in regularly. The iPhone that belonged to Von was part of the property, as well.

His car was out front. The keys were there in the house. The two DT's went through it also and discovered more electronic communication devices, in addition to illegal contraband. There was twenty pounds of weed and five thousand MDMA pills in the trunk.

"Looks like the guy had more going on than we initially thought, Valco" Bill acknowledged at the discovery of the material.

"Apparently so. Now we've got to find out what. Do we get a warrant for the women now or leave them be?" Valco responded.

Bill pondered deeply over the question. He was never the type of police, let alone man, to have the duty to help, then turned to do harm to a family.

"Nah. We don't want to pile more hurt and problems onto a family. I don't believe they knew anything about the underworld dealings of Alfredo. We leave it be. We don't even say anything to them about it. However, I do believe there is a family member or so, who's heavy into dealing. We've got to investigate them," Bill stated.

"And these devices we've got should definitely help us do the work."

"Absolutely should. Absolutely should, partner."

$$\$\$\$\$$

Chloe and Von entered the church to attend the funeral. They immediately located Rosa and her mother. The two approached and offered hugs. Chloe hugged her aunt first then Rosa, leaving her boyfriend to follow her lead. Rosa observed the order going on with Chloe from the hugs, and took two steps back to be out of ear shot of Chloe. She had something on her mind to say to Von. When he was to embrace her.

Von hugged the mother and expressed his sorrow for the loss. He then proceeded to do the same with Rosa. They wrapped tightly.

"I'm sorry for your loss, Rosa. I know you loved your brother and gonna really miss him," Von uttered.

Rosa buried her face and breasts into Von's chest area. She began to cry as they held one another. Passionate feelings of intimacy and desire filled her body, like they were wrapped tight and making love as if newlyweds on a honeymoon. She was falling in love with him. Probably faster than anticipated.

Rosa ran her hands all over Von's body, not taking into account that the guy's girlfriend was standing right there. Her cousin.

"You gonna be able to come by later? Please do. I need you there with me," Rosa whispered into his ear.

"I will. Just be cool, aight," he responded.

Chloe looked at the extended embrace of the two. Something in her woman's intuition was triggered. She knew the touch, the hug, the strong eye contact. The energy between Rosa and Von was beginning to tell on them. It was *undeniable*.

What the.... Chloe thought to herself as she looked on at Rosa and Von. Her mouth was slightly agape. She was shocked in a way.

Finally, Rosa let Von go and made eye contact with Chloe as if to say, *"he was yours, but he's mine now. That boy is mine, sweetie."*

They all then took their seats and went through with services.

After leaving the cemetery, Von and Chloe went back to their place prior to him leaving once the sun had gone down, Chloe asked him about the hug between he and her cousin.

"Ah, that wasn't nothing. She knew me and Alfredo had a bond through Tito. That's all that was," he lied.

"Oh, don't let me find out, Von. *Family off limits* with this open relationship thing I wanted to experience. This was the reason why I asked for that. It was really all about me considering you and not making you feel tied down."

"I know you're young and want to live a little. And I had to allow that. But we've got plenty of time to talk about it," Chloe stated.

Von looked at her with strong eye contact and then smirked.

"I hear you, Chloe. But we're good. Ain't no thing," he responded, then turned to walk out the door. He got into his rental and rode off.

He was in the processing of making a stop by Rosa's, a stop by Monyetta's, then meeting up with Cold Heart at Shayla's spot she had with Tangee.

There was no longer a threat. The nigga Feezy had been moved out the way. Von needed to speak with Cold Heart about it all since he was supplying the girls.

$$\$\$\$\$\$$$

With the conclusion that Alfredo's life was ended from a Black Rhino bullet through the mouth and out the back of his head, the federal investigation was building behind the information that Alfredo provided. Alfredo was a confidential informant and was looking to aid in the take down of Puerto Rican drug kingpins who sold hard drugs. The opioid epidemic in America was beginning to catch fire and spread out of control. Alfredo had gotten caught with multiple pounds of the weed they'd taken from Von, two thousand opioid pills, and the pistol Von had. He was in possession of a firearm while being a convicted felon, and in commission of a crime, trafficking weed and heroin laced pills. A mandatory twenty year minimum, unless... he cooperated. He did. Even ratted on Tito about certain things. But Bill and Valco had no clue of Alfredo informing.

Chapter 8

One Month Later…

Kidada was contact by her father's lawyer, Levi Jacobson. He'd updated her on his client's case, as Little Hound had specifically instructed his attorney to relate any and everything to his daughter because she had faster access to him than Levi would. Hound Jr. didn't want Levi to know anything about the cell phone he had. Dude was trusted but not with *everything* the former kingpin looking to become business mogul had going on.

Levi filed a "Motion To Vacate Void Judgment" in the court on Little Hound behalf. The objective was to bypass the Successive Habeas Corpus Process and have the original trial judge review the motion and surrender a decision. A hearing was requested, and the Honorable Judge J.E.B Eckard III, a federal high ruler appointed by President George W. Bush, would preside over the case. The judge who sentenced Hound Jr. long retired, leaving Eckard III to fill his seat and take over his caseloads. The best part about the connection between Eckard III and Levi was that the two attended law school together, were a part of the same secret society, and had a solid friendship. Levi reached out to the friend and needed a favor J.E.B. wanted 300K to overturn and rule in the way Levi needed him to, and Levi demanded 250 K for who he knew.

"In my world, Cornelius, a lot of times, it's not about *what* you know, per se. But rather *who* you know, that could move mountains and get things done in the way we want them to. Fortunately for you, I know somebody. You're lucky," Levi said to him on the attorney-client visit. "You're a very lucky man."

"I'm more than happy to know I'm a lucky man, Levi. And in *my* world, it's always a good thing to know people like *you*, who know other people who move mountains and get things done," Little Hound responded.

"Now here's the other part. My 'retainer fee' for this *'special service'* I now offer to you, is gonna cost a half million bucks plus fifty thousand dollars," Levi informed.

"I thought Damien already took care of everything?" Hound Jr. asked.

"He has. The first part got you on my client list. But the *other part,* the part I'm now speaking to you about, Damien know nothing about this. Only you and I. This situation I've now worked out for you, is the best fit. We're gonna bypass a lot of stuff to get you out. You want it or you don't? Take it or leave it?" stated Levi.

"Well of course you know I want it. Hell, I wanna go home!" Hound Jr said with a smile.

"Look, I've got it. Aight. Imma have my daughter come by with the money. But what's my chances here, Levi?"

The lawyer smiled gleefully at his client, refocused his eyes on the documents inside the open briefcase, and then looked back towards the federal inmate he had the obligation to represent.

"If I'm here telling you about it, Mister Savage, that mean your chances are very good, sir. Very good. I don't intend to disappoint you," Levi stated emphatically.

"I'm totally convinced, Mister Jacobson. I've never felt better. Let's do it."

The visit concluded not long after the assurance of his freedom by the lawyer.

$$$$$

Hound Jr. needed to get busy rounding up the $550k the lawyer needed to make magic for him and have the doors to the federal prison open. He had it, no doubt, but in three different locations. Von's mother, Lilly, held seven figures in cash for him, only those two knew about. Kidada's mom, Juanita, had seven figures in cash for him. And his father, Hound Sr., held seven figures in cash for him as well. All was left to do was have his eighteen year old daughter, Kidada, make a stop to see everyone and get the money. She was told that $200K from each person would be passed over to her, beginning with her grandfather then on to Lilly, then to Juanita. Kidada was not telling anyone that her father was on the verge of getting released soon. She was good at keeping things secret.

Chapter 9

The relationship Lilly and Bernard shared was not going well at all in the New Year of 2009. He came up short on the money for the bills that month, and this was the thing to totally do it for her. Indeed, she had the money and was very well capable of paying all her bills, in need of no man. And by Bernard not living up to his part, the decision became easier for her to cut ties and leave him be.

Two weeks before the day, Bernard saw his stuff was put out and the lock was changed. He didn't put up any argument or fight with her because he knew his expectations as her man and doing his part failed, and he'd felt he could make things right once he'd gotten the money, and the rift in their relationship would be repaired. Wasn't going to happen on Lilly's doorsteps.

Bernard stalked Lilly for the time he'd been out. He was a wreck of himself too. The drinking became outrageous. He popped depression pills like crazy, pain pills, and also did lines of cocaine to take his mind away from what he was going through.

On this particular day, Lilly didn't go to work. She and Jamar checked into a hotel suite to have some fun and do what they do, fuck like crazy, and keep one another entertained for the time they were together. It was a Friday and the idea was for them to spend the entire weekend with one another. They'd turn off their phones and didn't want to be bothered by no one, especially not Bernard for her.

Lilly didn't know it but Bernard followed her that day, from the moment she'd left her house to the point of her picking up Jamar to the point of those two checking into the Ritz-Carlton downtown. He was armed with a pistol, ill-will in his heart, and was intent on blowing out the brains of both Lilly and Jamar, and then turn the gun on himself to keep from being prosecuted. Bernard was suicidal and a dangerous man, unfit for society in general and himself as a whole.

As bad as he wanted to, Bernard couldn't just run up in the hotel, shoot Lilly and Jamar down like rabid dogs in the street, and then turn the gun on himself. He didn't know what room they were in, and too many people present who would witness his madness. He'd been provided a break. Lilly needed to make a run to her house, get a key to the mini safe she'd had tucked away at her mother's home, then go there to get money for her son's dad, and pass it to his daughter. The day was the day he'd asked her to do so. Lilly had $1.5 million in cash that belonged to her ex. He needed $200 K of it, as requested from her.

Bernard was seated in his sister's car outside the hotel. He'd jumped to action upon seeing Lilly's fire up and began pulling out the storied parking lot. He allowed her space to get four car lengths ahead of him. He had a good idea she was headed home, being she was by herself and driving in that direction. He was correct.

Lilly pulled up to her house, got out, and went inside. Bernard followed closely behind, parked down the street to not alert her, then fast-walked to the house. The night was just setting in.

Bernard took cover in the lawn shrub bushes next to the front door. Lilly was in and out in five minutes. While locking the door, Bernard jumped out of his hiding space.

"Where the fuck you think you're going, bitch?!" he barked. Bernard now had his gun trained on her.

"Ah! Bernard! Wha-what are you doing?" Lilly responded, her voice went from harsh and in the process of scolding him, to a low purring whisper at the sight of the gun and the insanity his eyes possessed. She was now paralyzed with fear.

"Shut the fuck you! And open that goddamn door!"

He gripped her up by the hair and pinned the gun to her head.

Lilly began to open the door again and trembled terribly bad from fear. She wet herself. Urine ran down her leg, onto her heels, down to the concrete porch.

"Bernard, please...please don't do this. Okay. I thought you loved me, and–"

"Bitch! Shut your goddamn mouth! I don't want to hear SHIT you gotta say now."

The door opened, and he pushed her inside down to the floor. He then kicked her in the chest with the bottom of his boot before he slapped her.

WHOP!

Bernard then closed the door, grabbed Lilly by the arm, and dragged her on the floor to the bedroom. Once inside, he gripped her hair with both hands and yanked her from left-to right, mopping the floor with her head. He wanted to talk. He began demanding to know why. Why did she dump him and give up on what they had? Why was she at the hotel with the other guy? Who was he? Why was she dogging him out so bad and didn't seem to consider hard times had honestly hurt him?"

Lilly did the best she could to answer Bernard's questions and plead for mercy at the same time. He sat on the bed with the gun still pointed.

Von had been extra busy trying to contact his mother all day long. Lilly had her phone on airplane mode and paid no attention to text messages. He'd been by on three separate occasions throughout the day and wasn't able to lay eyes on her. He'd asked Chloe was she at work that day? Chloe told him no, she wasn't. Von decided to go by once more for the day. Her car was there now, so he parked and got out.

"Bitch, why the fuck you played with my emotions?!" Bernard yelled in Lilly's face.

Von heard the emotional outburst.

What the fuck! Sound like that nigga, Bernard, Von thought to himself.

He tried to unlock the door knob. He noticed it was already unlocked. Bernard didn't lock it back. He'd forgotten.

Von eased the door open. It creaked. Bernard heard it.

"Who the fuck there?! I'mma blow this bitch's head off!"

Von hurried and closed the door, and then speed walked to the kitchen.

Bernard stood to his feet from the bed and made his way to the living room. He opened the door and spotted Von's rental. He then slammed the door with one hand and leveled his pistol with the other as he turned to try and locate where Von was, if he'd came inside.

BOOM!

A shot had been fired.

Bernard hit the floor face first with a hole in his forehead. He was dead as shit.

His body twitched and blood poured from his skull. Von had murked dude. He now claimed three killings at his hands. He only had the cops to deal with from there and explain things to. But what if he called his people and they get rid of the body first? It was too late for that now. His mother had already dialed 911 on the house phone when Bernard went to the door. She had the phone to her ear as she slowly walked to the front of the house.

"Baby, you okay? I'm on the phone with the 911 people," Lilly stated.

"Mom, hang up!" Von yelled.

Lilly did so. But it was far too late. By the call being placed initially, the cops were on the way.

Von put his gun back into his waistband and ran out the house. He got into the car and sped off.

Bernard was executed with a Black Rhino. An extremely lethal piece of ammo.

PART TWO

Chapter 10

Upon Von putting to death his mother's boyfriend with a headshot, he speedily exited the house, got into the rental car he drove, and made his way to the place he shared with Chloe, one of the three girlfriends he rotated between. She wasn't there, and he had the privacy to speak over the phone like he needed to while Chloe was at work.

Von used one of the many back-up-cell phones he had to call his mother. She was still there at her house where the body of Bernard lay. The cops was urged by 911 dispatch to do a check at the house. They had not arrived yet. But sirens could be heard in the background enough to know that they were on the way.

"Hello! Hello... Hello!" Lilly let out hysterically. She was in tears and at the point of a panic attack.

"Mom, it's me, Vonnie! Is the –"

"Baby! Baby! You okay? You somewhere safe?"

"I'm good, Mom. I'm good. Why the hell you call the cops for?"

"Vonnie, I didn't know you were there. He was gonna kill me, son. I had to hurry and call for help. There was no other choice," Lilly said to her son.

"Look, don't tell the cops nothing, a'ight. I ain't going to jail behind a loser, Ma! I mean it!"

"I don't know what else to tell them, son, what should I say?"

"Tell them you don't know who shot him! He went to answer the front door and some body-"

"Hey-Hey-Hey! The cops here now! I gotta go, okay. I love you, son," Lilly cut him off to say and quickly ended the call.

"Fuck!" Von exclaimed. He didn't have the opportunity to properly convey the lie he needed his mother to perpetrate to the police.

Four squad cars were now on the scene at Lilly's house. They hopped out with guns drawn and ready to shoot. The 911 operator heard the fatal gunshot and communicated to the police to proceed with lethal caution.

Lilly ran out the house with her hands held high.

"Police! Police! Freeze! Don't move! Get down on the ground or we'll shoot!" The cops barked at her.

"Okay-okay! Please don't shoot! The dead man in the living room! Please don't shoot!" She responded in a loud tone of voice, then began to lay chest first on the pavement.

Lilly was lucky the cops didn't began firing away at her when she ran out the house the way she had with her phone in the air. It was dark outside, and they could've easily misperceived her device for a weapon. They exercised proper judgment and didn't act too fast.

They approached her, put on a pair of cuffs as caution until they knew what took place, then put her in the back of one of the police cars. They then entered the house to see what the situation was. They were met at the door by a dead body one foot away from the swinging space opening. The crime scene and homicide units were then called upon. That meant Bill and partner Valco would have to show up. So much for a day off for the two.

$$$$

William Edward "Bill" Hilliard was at the bowling alley with his wife and two daughters enjoying a much needed family day out. One they'd not had an opportunity to share in quite a long time. When the text came through his work phone: *187 on Darien Street*, he knew the family outing had come to an end. Bill sent Valco a text to notify him and was intent to carry-on with his wife and kids until his sidekick appeared to pick him up from there.

Bill's wife, Michelle, saw him take a look at his phone and. A display of concern dashed across his face.

"You got a call, sweetie?" she asked.

"I do, baby. At an odd time too. I wanted this night off. It's our anniversary weekend, you know. But we got a homicide in my jurisdiction, One on Darien Street," Bill replied.

She gave him a hug and kiss. "Go ahead, sweetheart. Do what you gotta do. Me and the girls will be okay. You have a position to uphold, and a job to do. It goes with the territory." Michelle then kissed him once more.

Bill began melting like a warm loving and kind teddy bear while in the arms of his wife of thirteen years.

"I love you so much, Michelle," he let her know as he always did.

"And I love you too, Bill…" another kiss, "…to the moon and back. You called Valco to come pick you up? Or you want us to drop you off?" she asked, having been through the same thing a time or two before.

"You know I called on my Hispanic Mel Gibson to come pick up his version of Danny Glover, That I am to him. We consider ourselves the *Philadelphia* duo of *Lethal Weapon*. No matter what, we got each other backs, and we're gonna get the job done," Bill said, causing her to smile at his sense of humor.

He and Michelle let the kids know he had to leave early due to a work emergency. The girls were already familiar with the drill themselves. They knew the type of passion their father had about his job as a policeman and protector of the people he served. No qualms were made by them to Bill.

Roughly twenty minutes later, Valco pulled up in his Ford F-150 truck and he and Bill made their way to the scene of the killing.

The CSI unit and responding offices had the place wrapped with crime scene tape and were canvasing the interior of the house. Lilly had already been taken to police headquarters to be questioned. Once inside the home, Bill and Valco were approached by the officer in charge at the time, Sergeant Gavin Lowe, who briefed them. He was the same person with CSI at the landfill when Alfredo's body was discovered.

"We weren't able to get but so much out of the girlfriend of the victim here," said Lowe, pointing down at a dead Bernard sprawled out on the floor in a large pool of his own blood.

"So what we have here, a domestic dispute with one shooting the other?" questioned Bill as he squatted low to the body to have a good look at the face of the victim. Bernard had been turned over from his face to his back now.

"Damn!" exclaimed Valco. "He took a hell of shot to the forehead here."

There was a hole the size of a nickel just off center on the left side of Bernard's skull.

"Not hardly the case here, sir. According to the girlfriend, a Lillian Dietrich, the victim took her at gunpoint with that gun there," he pointed to Bernard's pistol that had slid about five feet away from his body, "dragged her to the backroom," he pointed to the skid marks on the white carpet made by Lilly's shoes, "and threatened to kill them both. He then made a break towards the front door under assumption someone was there. She claimed she heard a single gunshot and thought he'd committed suicide at that point. The 911 operator confirmed hearing a blast of gunfire then, the voice of the caller had someone to shout out to her, to ask was she okay. To be exact, a third person called out, "Mom! Hang up!" Then the female caller responded by doing so. 911 called but got no answer," informed Lowe

"So we got a mother, who's the girlfriend, a boyfriend who's now the victim, and a son, somewhere in between the mix?" asked Bill.

"Exactly! But no mention of the son by the mother who we have down at the station " confirmed Lowe.

"Which means she may be protecting him because he's the potential shooter," Bill theorized.

"Appears that way to me," Lowe cosigned on the thought.

"And who is the guy?" Valco asked.

"No identification confirmation right now. But the girlfriend says his name is Bernard Nichols," Lowe made them aware.

"That's a heck of a hole there," Valco observed. "I wonder what type of bullet? Any exit wounds?"

"Nope."

"And once the autopsy is performed, they'll be able to retrieve the projectile that took the life of this guy," Bill uttered.

"Absolutely will," confirmed Lowe.

"Alright. Have nine-one-one dispatch send me an email of the audio of the call. Y'all go ahead and get him to the medical examiner's office and wrap this up. Me and Canelo gonna go down to the station and see….Lillian?"

"Lillian Dietrich, sir," Lowe reinformed.

"Lillian Dietrich. Got it. We're gonna see what she have to say about all this. Hopefully, she's got something to share with us."

"You two may have better luck with her than we had," Lowe worded.

"Well if she doesn't, we can certainly find something to change her with, I'm sure," spat Valco.

"We definitely can do that. Lets go Val," Bill stated.

They then exited the house and was near Valco's truck when one of the policeman on the scene got their attention to come his way for a moment. He was off to the side, talking with a guy who'd not long arrived in a taxi. It was Jamar. He'd rung Lilly's number relentlessly while at the hotel but got no answer. He decided to check her house to see what the situation was. Her car was still in the driving space in front of the house.

"Excuse me, Lieutenant Hilliard, you may want to hear this," the officer said to Bill as he and Valco approached.

"Yeah, who do we have here? Did he see anything?" Bill asked.

"No sir, I didn't. How are you by the way?" Jamar asked. "I'm Jamar Kitchens, the boyfriend of the person who owns this house, Lillian Dietrich," he made them aware.

Bill and Valco took a look at one another to be clear they'd heard all the guy had said. They then snatched their pistols from the holsters on their waistline and threw down on Jamar. He was arrested and taken into the station himself now for questioning. Jamar had no idea what was going on and he was livid.

Chapter 11

Von called Cold Heart to let him know what had happened.

"Yo, what up, bro?" Cold Heart answered.

"Cold!" Von called out his name in a concerning tone.

Cold Heart had heard him like this before, so he knew it wasn't good.

"Yo, where the fuck you at, bro? I'm on my way to get you. I can tell by how you talking, shit ain't right," Cold Heart said to Von.

"I'm at me and Chloe's spot, bro. I had to pop another motherfucker, Cold."

"Just tell me when I get there, homie. Not over the phone. Leave your main phone home too. Grab one of your other lines."

"Aight. Hurry and come get me, bro. ASAP!" Von stated.

Cold Heart had already disconnected the call.

Shortly thereafter, the friend was there and was informed of all that had taken place.

Von gave him a brief rundown of what transpired at his mom's house nearly an hour earlier.

"Von, what the fuck were you thinking, bro? You couldn't have just popped that nigga in the leg, the gut, or some other spot? Why you had to dome call him?" Cold Heart asked.

"What was I supposed to have done, bro? The nigga had his banger out on mom. And when he turned around from the door, he was gonna shoot me. I had to get him first," Von declared.

"You didn't mention he had a gun too, bro."

"I didn't?"

"Nah, you missed that part. But your mom. What's up with her?"

"I don't know, bro. I'm still trying to figure out why did she call the cops?"

"You say the nigga had her helmed up in the backroom, right? She ain't know you was in the front, and she only did the first thing to come to mind to stop that psycho motherfucka. I can't blame her. She had to do what she had to do, bro," Cold Heart said.

"You right about that. Now the cops got mama down at the station putting her through the bullshit. But I'm sure they gonna clear her at some point soon."

"Yeah, they will. Once they got another suspect to focus on. What you gonna do about that part?"

"Shit, I don't know. I gotta do something though. Can't let Mom go down like that," Von declared.

"I know that's right. And it ain't but one thing to do. I gotta run all this shit by Drip and Monk too, Von. You know we got a protocol to follow. We structured now," Cold Heart made him aware.

'I know-I know-I know. We gotta tell them."

"Exactly. Shit gonna be a'ight though. We gotta let the process play out."

"If they don't let mom go by Monday, we know what it is from there, don't we?"

"Damn sure do. But where you trying to go? What you trying to do?" Cold Heart inquired.

"I know what I can do. Imma call my sister, Kidada, let her know what's up, and have her call down to police headquarters to find out the status of mom. I'm probably gonna be back and forth between Dada's crib and here," Von informed.

"And in the meantime, I'mma go by your mom's house and have a look. I'll call Drip and Monk after that to let 'em know."

"No doubt, bro."

"No doubt."

The two homies then dapped one another up and embraced strongly prior to exiting the house, getting into their cars, and going different routes. They both had a high level of uncertainty on what was to come.

$$\$\$\$\$\$$$

Meanwhile....

Down at police headquarters, Bill and Valco had Lilly in one of the interrogation rooms and Jamar in the other. They'd gotten plenty out of him about her, whether she was there all day and the time she'd briefly left the hotel to go home and was to return shortly, but he didn't about her son Trevon or "Vonnie," or about the relationship the two had.

Jamar's story checked out, with hotel surveillance to support all he'd stated. They had no choice but to release him from custody. But not before they were to thoroughly question Lilly and cross reference her story with that of Jamar and what they knew opposite of.

She was now surrounded by the two detectives on both her sides, as they were in the process of having at it with her, drilling with a serious thread of hardcore questions, determined to know all the facts.

"Well, Miss Lillian Dietrich. How are you? I'm homicide detective, Lieutenant Bill Hilliard, and my longtime partner, Valente Canelo. I wanna begin by saying I'm sorry for your loss—"

"No need to have sorrow about Bernard. He wasn't a loss of mine," she cut Bill off mid-sentence to say. "Maybe a loss for his family but not one for me."

She had no love nor regard for her ex-boyfriend.

"Okay… Now we're past that part. You wanna tell us something we don't know already?" asked Bill.

"I've told you everything there is to know."

"No, you didn't," Bill challenged.

"The *other* boyfriend did… Jamar," Valco chimed in. He caused Lilly to jar her head in shock at the revelation.

"Jamar!" she retorted, attempting to play dumb.

"Yeah… *'Jamar Kitchens'*... the guy you played hooky from work to be with at the hotel. But that's not our problem. The guy you were with moments before you left to go home for whatever your reason was. And the guy you had intentions to be with, once you were able to get Bernard out the way. So, you had someone to kill the guy….A hitter, or your son!" Bill then barked, starling her in the process.

"Ha! That's crazy! Why would I need to hire someone to kill a man I already had out of my life? Help me understand that… if you don't mind," Lilly pushed back.

"Have a listen to this, please ma'am," responded Bill.

He then played the 911 recording of the call she'd made. Lilly was reminded of all she'd said.

"Now…you wanna tell us more about your son? Where can we find him? And allow us the opportunity to question him. Or do we need to issue a warrant for the arrest of Trevon Dietrich-Savage, and have him brought in for that process to take place? Have it your way, ma'am," Bill stated emphatically.

"Look man…You leave my son out of this, okay. If you wanna take anybody down for this killing…Let it be me. Okay," she responded.

"I can't do that, 'Momma Bear'! You're *not* the killer. We have strong reason to believe *your son* is. That he did it for *you.* And then planted that gun on the victim to make it appear that Bernard had it to kill you. Any jury in the country would eat this up, hook-line-and sinker. Then bury you *and* your son, in prison… *for life!* Him for the murder, and you as a partner to a crime. You wanna talk now?" Bill had gotten serious as ever with her now.

Lilly began to cry and tremble terribly. She didn't know what could be said to have them keep away from her beloved son. She needed to think of something. And fast.

Bill began talking to her once more. "Look Lilly, I've been doing this long enough to know what happened in that house, okay. Why won't you make this process a lot easier on yourself and on your son? Because just as sure as shit stinks, with him armed and still at large, riding around out there in a black on black Dodge Magnum Jamar told us he had, and the one we seen him standing beside in those photos in your living room...Only the worst could happen when we go after him to arrest. Only the worst! I promise you. Now go on ahead and tell us where we might be able to locate him, if you will? Don't make this no harder than it have to be. Please. I beg of you," Bill did his best to urge her about the information he needed. Valco jarred his head at something Bill let out in speech to Lilly. Bill took notice of his partner's demeanor.

"What's that look all about, Valco?" he asked.

Valco called him to the side and pointed to a page in his writing pad where he wrote down a few notes. He then said something to him in a whisper.

"Black Dodge Magnum, Bill. A young guy by the name *'Von'* was mentioned by the eyewitnesses Flowers and Moore, who saw the guy, Lassiter, shot and killed on eighth and Diamond," Valco brought to Bill's recollection.

"Oh yeah! That's right. I'd forgot all about that. I'm glad you didn't though, partner. Damn, I thank you for that," Bill expressed.

"A small world, ain't it?" Valco remarked.

"A *very* small world, brother. Very small. We can also question him about that too. Once we have our witnesses identify him in a line-up," stated Bill.

"We headed in the right direction, aren't we?"

"The absolute right direction. Now all we gotta do is go out and nab Von. We've got two killings we'd like to know about now," Bill confirmed, then made his way back to Lilly.

"Okay, we are waiting to hear more from you there, Lilly," Bill commented.

"Oh, you are? Okay. I no longer want to go on with this interrogation, I wanna speak with a lawyer," she stated, then was as quiet as can be.

"No problem. Have it your way. Lillian Dietrich, you're now under arrest for the murder of Bernard Nichols. You have the right to remain silent. Anything you say, can and will be used against you in a court of law..."

"Wait! NO! You can't do this! I ain't shoot no one!" Lilly protested to no avail.

Bill began putting the cuffs on her behind her back in real police format. She was about to be taken to the Philadelphia County Jail facility and booked on malice murder charges. There was nothing she could do.

The two investigators then went back over their questions from before with Jamar. They'd gotten a little bit more out of him from all he'd been told by Lilly, about her son, their family, and her son's father's family. They then pulled the profile of the father and began to have a better understanding of who Lilly and her son were. They had a lot more to work with from that point.

The hunt for Von was now more urgent than previously.

Chapter 12

Three Weeks Later...

Drip had Von and Cold Heart meet up with him at the home he had in Montgomery County. Monk was already there two hours early, long before the two arrived. He wanted to be brought up to par on the whole situation about the shooting there in person and not over the phone.

Von's mother, Lilly, was still being held without bail, and now they had to do everything necessary to get her attorney to do what they could to have bond granted on her behalf. She wasn't talking to them, and they were making her feel the pain and agony of her decision to keep quiet about the shooting. She was so serious about protecting her baby.

The police did not issue a warrant for Von's arrest until two weeks after the fact. Drip found this out through the lieutenant police that he had on payroll. He made Drip aware that there was not one but *two* arrest warrants for little Vonnie. For questioning though. Nothing more. Drip began with what he had to say to Von.

"Little fam, we got a serious situation brewing with you in the city. And not only that, your mom still looked up. What the fuck, Vonnie?" Drip said.

"I know fam, I know. But bro. Truth be told, I had no choice but to put dude in the dirt, Drip! The nigga was about to kill moms! He would have killed me, had I not popped his ass first! I had to, Drip," responded Von.

"No doubt. I'm aware of the situation. I sent one of my lawyers to go and talk with her. She told them everything that happen. But the only reason they're still holding her is because they looking for you. To question. And once they lock you up, they're gonna let Lilly go more than likely."

"I know, bro. And I gotta get Mom out at all cost. But I don't understand why the cops are dragging her with no bail?"

"They're gonna eventually give her one. She just gotta go to a higher judge to be granted that right. That'll happen after about sixty days. But in the meantime, you got somewhere not in Philly to lay low. You need to get all the way out the way, Vonnie. Seriously."

"No. I don't, bro. I mean fam, I don't."

"No problem. I've got a spot up in Williamsport you can stay. Once we get this whole shit worked out, then you can come back to the city, fam. It's money to be made up there too. I want you to work an angle. While you are there, make a way to sell products. You got a couple dudes you can take with you to help establish the hustle there?" Drip asked.

Von looked at Cold Heart for him to help think of a few other guys that he could call on to go upstate PA with him. Actually, they both had three in mind. They were Ron, and his two wild-ass outlaw cousins, Khaddafi and Khalil. Once they'd properly made an imprint, Von could then have the girls go back and forth between there and Philly, Shayla, Tangee, and Cori. He revealed to his people who he wanted and who he could get to tag along with.

"Yeah, I've gotta couple people we could rotate in and out of the Williamsport spot. How soon do you need me to head that way, fam?" Von asked.

"Vonnie, the cops got your mom locked up as a party to the crime of murder. They looking for you to question about that. More than likely, they'll eventually charge you for that too. How soon do you really think you need to get the fuck outta Philly?" Drip started with a serious tone to his voice.

"Shit, ASAP! Like tonight."

"Exactly," remarked Drip. He then withdrew a set of keys from his pocket to hand over to Von.

"Here. You gonna need these. Also, how much work you got left from that last batch of supply?" asked Drip.

"It's about two units," Von responded.

"Take that with you. And I'm sure you got a female you can take along until your homies you got in mind could join, right?"

"Cori, Von." Cold Heart quickly chimed in.

"This the perfect opportunity to know what she all about. She's always on your dick trying to throw the pussy on you and shit! You can now work the shit outta her. We're gonna need Shay and Tangee to keep up the good work at the spot." Cold Heart stated.

"That's the same shorty who you had with you that night, Cold?" Body had asked, using a finger to trace a line on his face from ear to the nose, indicating the cut Shayla had. Body was using the bathroom when they arrived. He now was part of the conversation.

"Yeah, she one of them, bro. The Cori broad her sister," Cold Heart confirmed.

"Gotcha, bro. I'm understanding."

Body remembered the name of the female who'd popped the dude he had tied in the trunk of the car.

"She's the one I had in mind anyway, bro. The other females I deal with are not in the streets like that anyway so yeah, I've got a girl, fam… she's down for the cause," Von said.

"Okay, cool. I'm sure Cold there will be able to hold down the crew y'all got in the city for the time being and keep it moving with the product. Before long, everything should be good to go. But until then, this is how we are going about business. And little fam, keep your ass up there in Williamsport until I tell you it's cool to come back to Philly. Don't do so without my permission, aight. I mean that shit, fam. We got enough clean-up work to do already. Don't need no more," Drip stated emphatically.

"I understand, fam. I got you on that," Von replied humbly.

They all then got up from their seats and exited the home. Von and Cold Heart got into Monk's car with him, and Drip and Body took Drip's gray colored Range Rover. The both of them were headed to the city as well. Back to the penthouse, then to a mature social spot to party. Afterall, it was Friday.

$$$$$

The property Drip owned in Williamsport was actually a small farm with a brick home and a wooded area behind the eight acre estate. He had a few livestock animals there as well (cows, pigs, chickens, and goats), with an older Hispanic guy who was paid to keep them fed and the grass cut. This farm operated as a getaway location for Drip when he needed a temporary break. But Drip was all about the hustle and making money with drug deals and all else. He simply could not refuse the chance to find a way to exploit the underworld of the small Pennsylvania town, the site of the yearly Little League Baseball World Series. Von would be the one to serve the purpose of putting Drip's products down on the streets there.

Once back in Philly, Von went straight to the house he and Chloe had to begin packing for his trip upstate. She was home and wanted to talk.

"Vonnie, look, okay," she began while sitting on the bed, watching a movie, and looking at Von pack a few things.

"I've seen the news; I've read the paper, and I've heard more than enough at work about what's going on with your mom. Not to mention her being absent from work. But I need to know directly from you, baby…What in the hell happened, and what's now going on? You can't keep holding this away from me, Von. You can't. It's not right. I've been here by your side for two years now, and also, your mom's my friend. So talk to me. Please," Chloe begged him.

Von stopped what he was doing then and there, took a seat on the bed, locked eyes with Chloe, and then went on to tell her everything. He'd came to realize at that point how much he needed her in the situation. He could have Chloe visit his mother and relate messages between the two. So, being truthful about it all was a must. Lying to Chloe would only complicate this more.

In addition to the information about the shooting, he let his main lady know where he was on his way to and what the plan was at that point. Chloe, being very understanding to a high degree as she was, accepted Von's silent plea for her help and promised not to abandon him or his mother.

Von then gave Chloe a key to his mother's home, to go and clean up the place. No one had been there since the shooting and the intense search he knew they'd conducted.

"It can't be too bad. They only wanna question me about it. Not arrest me for murder. So… It's bad but not that bad. I'll survive it," Von swore.

"That sounds better. Come here. Let me help ease some of the emotional pain and take your mind away from that for a moment. Wanna put it on me since you're gonna be gone from me for a little while," stated Chloe as she brought her body close him and began caressing his chest and kissing on his neck.

The two hadn't enjoyed one another sexually in a few weeks, and that moment proved to be a good instance to do so. Chloe was ready and so was Von. They tongue-kissed and began to get naked. From there, Chloe initiated the action, and they'd gotten all the way into it at that point. A sexual release was something very much needed by the both of them.

Chapter 13

Bill and Valco managed to have a lot of success in their investigative efforts of not one, but *three* homicides that had the same type of evidence, and all involving one person who they could place at the scene of the crime of each. That person was Trevon Dietrich Savage, the son of Lilly Dietrich and Cornelius Savage II.

How so? The shell casing found at the location where Bernard was killed matched the one found at the location where Kavon Lassiter lost his life. And also, the one found at a home in southwest, where an eyewitness reported hearing a single gunshot come from a garage and then seeing two cars exiting, with one being a black Dodge Magnum, the same type of vehicle the police put out an APB on and related through the news for citizens to be on the lookout for one that had a broken left headlight. The home that the shot was heard fired from was no longer occupied. A half cleaned blood stain was discovered, along with that third casing. A *Black Rhinos.*

The bullets retrieved from Bernard and Lassiter in the autopsy matched ballistically. And the DNA from Alfredo's blood was the same as that found on the concrete floor of the garage in the home in Southwest.

The detectives were able to link Von to the three killings because his cell phone pinged at each location around the time the homicide happened. The *Verizon* towers recorded the data and was able to be gathered by Philly Homicide. Not to mention the 911 records revealed him there at one, two eyewitnesses—Tobias Flowers and girlfriend identified him at the other—and his car—the same seen at a shooting scene—was reported at the last—from the strongest of evidence to the least strongest.

Lilly's house and cell phone records were seized, alone with the cell phone itself. Bill secured a warrant to hack into it and discovered Von's contact information inside. Lucky for Bill, one particular number was also found in phone records of other persons of interest in pending murder investigations. Von's status was upgraded from *"wanted for questioning"* to *"wanted for murder."* A task force was sent out to try and nab him, and they started with his grandmother's house. Police only had one problem with it all. They didn't know what Von looked like. He had no record nor any mugshots. It helped in a major way in that regard, especially since he didn't have a driver's license yet. How lucky was he.

BOOM!

The force of the battering ram used by the police had knocked the door clean off its hinges of Mrs. Edna Dietrich's nice Germantown home. It was in the wee hours of the morning, around three thirty a.m.

"Freeze old lady! Don't you move! Get your hands up or we'll shoot!" The lead squad officer demanded.

He then yanked the old lady from the bed by the arm and forced her to the floor.

"Ah! What are you people doing to me in my own home?" Mrs. Edna protested in agony.

The officer was performing a tactical move on her while putting on a pair of cuffs. He had his knee in her back and spread her legs to rough her up. He was an overweight guy and held back none. H was totally abusing his authority.

Once Mrs. Edna was secured and held in place, the many squad officers then searched her home, storming through and looking for anyone else in the house, weapons, and contraband. The warrants for a murder suspect provided ultimate power.

The police located no other person and discovered nothing illegal in the old ladies' domain.

"Where is your grandson, ma'am?" Bill asked Mrs. Edna upon him now entering the home. The warrants were executed in his capacity and command.

"Trevon Dietrich Savage, his name, correct?" asked Bill. "The son of your daughter we have in custody, Lillian Dietrich?"

"That's my grandson, sir. But I haven't seen him in quite awhile now. I don't know where he's at. He only comes by every so often, not much. Now, you people need to turn me loose, I'm not guilty of anything. Take these things off my arms. They hurt," Mrs. Edna argued.

"Cut her loose," Bill ordered. "We've got nothing on her."

The officer who'd put the cuffs on her now took them off. They were in process of going to the next location in search of the suspect.

It was a good thing Lilly had the cash she was holding for Von's father in a secure spot at her mother's home. It was in the laundry room outback of the house in a small shed under the dryer in a safe. They'd missed it by not bothering the building, so she'd caught a break. Something that was needed for them and the predicament she found herself in.

In addition to the search of Mrs. Edna's home, the detective duo–Bill and Valco–made it to their vehicle to contact the DMV and had them provide a list of all the people who owned a black colored Dodge Magnum. The list of names were easily narrowed to the home of Mrs. Edna. Lilly had her last name. Objective achieved. Problem was, they didn't locate the vehicle at the residence either. They were in the hopes of finding it at the next stop they were set to raid. The apartment on Cottage Street where Von and Chloe lived.

BOOM!

The door to the place was broken down. No one was there. Chloe and her family was in Puerto Rico burying a loved one. Her grandfather had passed away, and they were on the island mourning his death.

They tore the place apart and left the warrant on the dining room table.

The Magnum had been repaired and was driven now by "Cori" on a needed basis by word from Von. He had it put away in a storage shed. He and Cori were the only two who knew and had access to it. Everything was going good for Von and he was out of harm's way.

$$\$\$\$\$\$$$

The lawyer for Little Hound, Levi Jacobson, was present in court with his inmate-client alongside him. The hearing request was granted by the judge presiding over the case, JEB Eckard III, and the moment was at hand to argue the error presented.

In the spectator section sat Kidada, her grandfather Big Hound, her mother Juanita, Big Hounds' wife Henrietta, and Drip and one of his young girlfriends, Divida Anderson, a young, beautiful, butter pecan complexioned African-American sweetheart who was majoring in business and account management at Penn. She was twenty years of age and was on the volleyball team at the Ivy League school as well. She was very lovely.

The judge called the court to order.

"All rise…" announced the bailiff. "The Honorable Judge JEB Eckard the third preside."

"You may be seated. This is a hearing for a new trial, in the case of Cornelius Aaron Savage the second versus the United States of America. Who is counsel representing Movant?" the judge asked. Basically going through the formalities of proceedings.

"I am, Your Honor. Levi Jacobson, the attorney on record," he stood to state.

"And counsel representing the government?"

"That'll be me, You Honor. AUSA Cooper Gordon," stated the tall, red head, rail thin, male attorney who had a crew cut and freckles on his face. He'd gained an aggressive approach through many years in the military. Cooper was a Marine veteran.

"Very well. This is your motion, Mister Jacobson. You want to open up with it at this time?" stated the judge.

The legal proceedings continued with both attorneys going back and forth as to why the convictions should be set aside and why they shouldn't. But little to AUSA Gordon's knowledge, the ruling Jacobson sought was already paid for. It showed that power and influence had a serious way of being worked from an angle of an unseen hand.

The hearing lasted for nearly three hours then concluded. Judge Eckard III didn't make a ruling then and there. He announced he needed to receive the briefs filed and the transcript from the hearing. Maybe three months. Maybe six months. Maybe a year. Nonetheless, a ruling shall come.

Little Hound had been housed at the FDC on 6th and Market over the weekend. He would be transferred back to Coleman FCI the upcoming Monday. The family all paid him a visit. Everyone except his beloved son, Trevon. Drip and Kidada made him aware of the entire situation. Little Hound had a reason to panic in a way. Lilly held over a million in cash that belonged to him; and he needed her out of jail. Drip let him know it wouldn't be too much longer before she's granted bail and that he was going to do all he can to hold it together for him. Little Hound took Drip on his word. Besides, he owed him a huge favor anyway. One that Drip would spend the remainder of his life paying off.

$$$$$

Von contacted Monyetta. He had her make a trip by his grandmother's house to check on her. He couldn't call because he read that the cops would be listening in and track the call to his location in Williamsport, something he didn't need.

While Monyetta was there with Mrs. Edna, she had Von on the phone. He needed to speak with his grandma.

"Nana, it's me, Vonnie," he said to her.

"Baby. Hey, you okay?" Mrs. Edna responded.

"I am, grandma. How about you?"

"The cops came here and destroyed my home."

"Huh!" he exclaimed. Von had no knowledge that she was raided.

"They say they are looking for you, baby. Nana too old for all this, Vonnie. What's going on? And when they plan to let your mom out of that God-forsaken place?"

"Momma should be out soon. And this whole mess will be over and done with before long, Nana."

"Lord knows I hope so. I need Lilly here to take me to the grocery store and to help out around the house, Vonnie. My daughter's been in there almost a month now. We got to make this situation right, baby."

"I know, Nana. And we will. My girlfriend there with you now, gonna make it her business to take you to the supermarket and check on you daily, okay. You okay with that, Monyetta?"

"No. I don't have a problem with that, Von. I'm okay with it. You're my dude now. And I've got to hold you down. We in this for the long haul, baby," Monyetta stated and assured Von where her loyalty lies.

"I love it when you talk like that, Monyetta. It lets me know you're with me without doubt."

"And you know I am, sweetie… I'm all the way with you there. Now Nana too," Monyetta said, smiling at Mrs. Edna at the same time.

They continued to talk a little longer then Von let them go so Mrs. Edna could be taken grocery shopping. He knew he had a winner in Monyetta.

$$$$

Von also had Monyetta visit the county jail and relay his words to his mother. She also let Lilly know that it would be her, to help out with her mother, Mrs. Edna, and do the part with the elderly lady, something once done by her prior to lock-up. Lilly thanked her dearly. She now had an additional friend in Monyetta, the same as she maintained with Chloe. Lilly simply shook her head in amusement at the polygamous activity of her son.

That boy is just like his daddy, Lilly thought to herself while looking on at Monyetta through the glass. She admired Vonnie for having his way with the females at an early age.

Chapter 14

Bill and Valco were doing follow-up work on the cases they had. They were busy making calls, visiting with family members of victims, and jail visits as well. The one case they had on their mind the most was that of the little girl, Dedra, being killed. The shooting victim's father, Feezy, seemed to have fallen off the face of the earth, as he hadn't been seen, heard from, or mentioned of in quite awhile. Each time the duo contacted little Dedra's mother, Esha, she appeared to be worried about Feezy now, as he was not contacting her at no time of the day. Bill and Valco were going there to check on her and listen when she called for him. They wanted to be sure that she wasn't lying on no accord and decided to stop by her apartment at the Fair Hill Projects on a surprise visit.

Knocking on the door, Esha was home. She answered and opened it let them inside.

"I wasn't expecting you two. What a surprise! I'm hoping you got something to tell me," stated Esha.

"We were hoping to find Stephon here. We haven't gotten any feedback from him at all. You know where we can locate him?" asked Bill.

"I haven't seen or heard from him. His mother hasn't either. Whoever it was that killed my baby and tried to kill him, must have doubled back and finally got him."

Esha had a somber tone to her voice, tears in her eyes, and hurt on her face. She was a destroyed woman.

"We didn't come to deliver the news of his death, ma'am. And we don't have his body down at the morgue. We thought maybe he was here, but we see he's not," Bill responded.

"No sir, he's not. And I'm guessing your investigation hasn't been going so well?" Esha asked.

"No ma'am, it hasn't, to tell you the truth. We're gonna continue to do all we can in this case, ma'am. And not going to be backed down until a significant arrest is made," Bill promised.

"What do you mean by a *'significant arrest?'* Has there been at least *one* made?" She asked.

"There has," confirmed Bill. "But he doesn't fit the bill of the shooter. We've got more investigating to do. Gonna go down to the county jail to question the guy yet again. He probably got something to tell us now since he's been there for a couple months with no bail."

"I'm hoping he does too. And why you're at it, you may want to go and question the so-called girlfriend Feezy was with at the time."

Valco flipped the page on his notepad and asked Esha a question. "That's that *'Shayla Allen'* girl you mentioned to us before?"

"Yes sir. That'll be her," she confirmed.

Valco placed a check mark next to the name written in his notepad. He then wrote down the words: *Shayla Allen," a female acquaintance of Richardson. "Baby girl" mentioned by Washington, has the same number found in the call log of both individuals. Could this be the same person?* Valco documented.

"We'll be in touch, Miss Davis. You have nice day, ma'am," concluded Bill

"You too."

The detectives then exited the apartment and made their way back to the unmarked government car, en route to interview J-Dubb once more.

$$$$$

Bill and Valco arrived at the county jail where J-Dubb was being held. They had him in the interview room putting him through another series of questions. J-Dubb had dried out and was forced to go cold turkey from his heroin addiction. He looked a ton better in weight, and his health had improved. Maybe he was less difficult to deal with now than he was when they'd brought him in.

"How are you doing, Mister Washington? Nice to see you again," Bill let out.

"Nice to see you too. And now I'm sure these phony charges y'all got me on gonna be dropped, right?" J-Dubb said in a mild polite tone.

"We're almost at that point, Johnny. But first thing first…we've got to clear you fully and be sure you didn't have any part in the shooting of a little girl that got killed, man. And I take it seriously because I have two daughters myself. And I'm affected by that," Bill responded.

"Look detective, a'ight. For the one hundredth time, and hopefully the last, I-ain't-no-god-damn killer, dude. Not in the least! I ain't shoot nobody! Not even with a water pistol! Okay. Now I appreciate your concern for me and my dope addiction and putting me through county jail rehab and shit. But dammit, it's time to go. Y'all wrong on charging me, it's time to go. Y'all wrong for charging me with murder and holding me this long. Turn me loose, man!" J-Dubb did his best to urge them to order his release.

"We'll get to that part. I promise. But we gotta know who had your car that day, Johnny? Because whoever it was had something to do with the shooting or know something about it," Bill responded.

"And who exactly is, *Baby Girl*, listed in your contacts in your phone?" Valco chimed in to ask J-Dubb.

"Baby girl is my dealer, man. She's the one and only person who I've ever let drive my car. And I can tell you now, she ain't have shit to do with no shooting! Dope being shot, yeah! But a guy and a kid getting killed…nah. That ain't her," J-Dubb stated and shook his head vehemently from side to side in protest to defend Baby Girl.

"What's her name now? What you call her?," Bill asked. "And her phone number is also in the call-log of one of the shooting victims."

"I don't know, man, 'She-She'…'Shay-shay'… Some shit like that. Hell, I don't know. All I know is she keeps some good ass dope."

"Crack or Heroin? "asked Bill, seeking clarity.

"Heroin! Dope! Smack! Boy! China White!" Blurted J-Dubb. He continued.

"Crack does nothing for J-Dubb," he said emphatically crossed his arms, then sat back in his seat b-boy style.

"Would *Shayla Allen* be her name?" asked Valco.

"Yeah! Something like that. The first name. I don't know about the last. We go by nicknames and first names in the streets. Y'all two know that," J-Dubb let out. "And by the way, now that I'm able to think about it. The day y'all say the shooting took place—a few days before Christmas--me and a female friend of mine, Tina McDaniels, were at the *Red Roof Inn* up in northeast Philly by the Franklin Mills Mall all that week. I reserved the room in my own name too. So make sure you go and check that. You can release me at this point," J-Dubb stated confidently.

Valco documented all of this, then began preparing an email to their secretary for a check to be made at the motel to confirm J-Dubb's story.

They then ended the interview. Now the duty for them was to find out exactly who was the Shayla Allen female whose name had been mentioned more than enough to question her. The focus of the case began to shift that day.

$$$$$

Meanwhile...

In upstate Pennsylvania—Williamsport—Von settled in pretty good and managed to get motion going with his heroin hustle. He'd been provided fake I.D cards and all the necessary to avoid any mishaps he may have been subjected to run into with police or another form of authority. Von basically had a totally new identity itself and lived a little different there than he had in Philly. He was *Tayshown Jefferson* now (or simply "TJ"). Drip had a packet of credentials he passed over to Von. He had a person on payroll who worked at the DMV. One of the females that Drip dealt with, Kerri Porter, whom worked at City Hall and provided Drip with information about the Warren guy. Her sister, Morgan, was the inside person.

Von and Cori locked in with each other in a beneficial way. She was allowed to continue driving his car, as he had her back and forth from Philly to where he now resided. And anytime the Magnum wasn't in use, she had to park it in the storage like he told her to. Cori proved to be the down ass loyal female he hadn't thought she would turn out to be. He thought maybe she was only into wanting to fuck him and suck him off good, then leave it be. But Cori shown and displayed differently all together.

Cori's duty was to deliver money to Monk that the crew in Williamsport had made. and keep Shayla and Tangee in line when they were getting money at her place and the house that Shayla and Tangee shared together. The threat of Feezy was no more, so they didn't have to sell their product at the location in West Philly any longer. Lonnie and Kareem continued to operate on that side of town and had added helping hands to the crew with the inclusion of a few family members and homies of theirs, leaving the girls able to get money in the territory they knew best.

Von had Cori get an apartment in her name for them in Williamsport. This was the place they shared anytime she was in town with him, mostly throughout the week.

Monyetta enjoyed him every other weekend, then Chloe, and he needed to find a way to work Rosa into the rotation. Talking about a dude who had his hands full with females. Von was him.

It was a Sunday night with Von and Cori having been together throughout the particular weekend, and she was on the verge of hitting the road to head back to Philly to deliver money to Monk for him. Von managed to keep it all business with Cori for the most part, and they hadn't fucked as of yet. He'd only allowed her the chance to give him head once, being she'd popped all that shit about how good she was at the art. She showed up and showed out. Impressive to say the least. And now her and Von were laid up in an apartment that they shared together, she was ready to take things a step farther between them and put the pussy on him. Like she'd always desired to do for far so long now but never got him to give in to her advances. That particular night produced something different in Von and he was ready to go with the program, so Cori popped it off.

Von was seated on the bed in a wife-beater and boxer shorts watching an episode of *The Wire* when Cori got out of the shower and exited the bathroom with a towel wrapped around her body and a few beads of water dotted on both shoulders. She then stood in front of the TV for Von to have a good look at her and all there were to offer.

Cori grooved and gyrated her hips and body to a tune of music that played in her mind and began to make herself appealing to Von in a special way. He then changed the channel on the TV to a music station. A track by R. Kelly was playing. It was his song *'Chocolate Factory'* from the *Chocolate Factory* album. Coincidently, Cori was one of those females who was obsessed with the successful R&B singer. She loved herself some R. Kelly and began to sing along to the lyrics of the song.

She then began talking to Von while enticing him with dance moves and peeling the towel from her body.

"Look at *all* this sexy body of mine that now belongs to you, Von… but the real question is, what do you plan to do with it? If you can handle it," she let out in a seductive tone as she allowed the towel to hit the floor, fully revealing her beautiful naked body.

She had a luscious set of 34 C-Cup breasts, 26 inch waist, and a 38 inch hips, thighs, and ass. Her skin was golden brown and glistened from the baby oils she'd used prior to coming out the bathroom. She ran her hands all over her breasts and body as she continued to slow dance and stimulate Von to the point she needed him to be pinching her nipples and running two fingers in and out of her love hole here and there.

Cori then turned and had her backside facing Von. She bent over to touch her toes, palmed the floor, and locked her hands around her ankles to twerk and jiggle her ass cheeks for the young buck. His dick was now rock hard and was standing straight up in attention.

"Damn, Cori! I never knew I've been passing all that up. You nice! I definitely like all I see," Von said to her. He'd finally began to respond like she wanted him to.

It was time for her to get aggressive with him like her nature called for.

"Nigga, I ain't the one for all that talking. Show me what you mean. Don't tell me about it," Cori spat, now challenging Von to be the shit at life he spoke of as it related to their acquaintance.

"You ain't gotta tell me twice," he uttered, then sprung from the bed to his feet and grab hold of Cori from behind.

She shook and twerked her ass against his manhood while he rubbed on her breasts and finger-fuck her from behind. Her thick juices coated his digital stimulators, provoking action for her.

Cori turned to face Von. Her light brown eyes mesmerized him. Von had never truly observed how gorgeous she honestly was. And now he had an eye full of her exotic features. They locked lips and tongue-kissed in a passionate, intense way. At the point of pausing to catch their breaths, Cori smiled at him. Her teeth were white and had nice structure to them, a quality many would never expected a product of a Philly ghetto to have. She then pushed him to the bed playfully and prepared to straddle him once he'd gotten naked himself. He was taking off his shirt while she looked on, then lowered his boxers. Cori went down on Von and took him in with a deep-throat. She then bobbled up and down slowly, utilizing her lips to tightly grip and execute a pull action with them.

"Ooh God! Damn this shit feels so good, Cori! You *do* know what the fuck you doing, don't you?" Von let out. "I'mma fuck around and fall in love with you, sweetheart."

She paused with her head job momentarily. "That won't be a bad idea. Hopefully after the night, the decision to do so would be easier for you."

She got back to work.

"It may… It just may," Von responded, then tilted his head to the back and enjoyed the moment.

Cori then got atop him, pressed her titties on his chest, began kissing him, and using her hand to grab hold of his dick, sitting the head at the entrance of her goodie box. She sat back and allowed his manhood the leeway to slide inside her. Cori began to ride him and gave Von a hell of an experience. They had no condoms and did not care for any. They both wanted it raw and uncut, just as they were.

"Come on… I want you to get this pussy from the back," Cori let out, then got on all fours atop of the bed.

Von got to his knees, palmed her ass cheeks with both hands, and spread them wide while penetrating. He began to slow stroke then pick up the pace. He fucked Cori hard and convincingly, smacking her on the ass here and there, and even leaning down to lick her pussy and booty hole in the process. She loved his sexual behavior.

Von was at the point of climax. He fucked and fucked and fucked, banged and banged and banged, until he couldn't hold back any longer. Little bro exploded his load deep inside Cori. He damn near passed out from the work he'd put in. Dude could do nothing but roll over on the mattress until his hearing returned and powered up to go again. Cori giggled and smiled at him, then placed her head on his chest.

"That was *everything* I thought it would be, Von. I've gotta have it again before I go," Cori complimented.

"Shit, what's the hold up! Let's get to it then, baby," he responded, then allowed her no more time to rest.

His dick was brick solid and erect. It never went down. He was built to go.

Chapter 15

Back In Philly...

Tito found himself very pissed behind the fact that somebody viciously murdered his cousin Alferdo or ordering that hit, and they had no idea who did it. He and the other family members who wanted something to happen behind it; they speculated and attempted to narrow down the list of potential perpetrators but were unable to pinpoint exactly who.

Tito had Raul, Enrique, Jamie—another cousin and worker of Tito who was part of the crew that robbed Von and Cold Heart—and a few others at his shop to question them and have them tell him about all the things they'd done behind his back to other people, so he could have an idea of who may have retaliated and killed Alfredo, and could possibly come at them next, or worst of all, at himself. He had good reason to believe some of those there actually did rob his cousin Chloe's boyfriend and paid him what they owed behind the selling of the material taken from Von, but he didn't know for certain. Honestly, that was the main thing he wanted to know. They all knew if Tito found out they were lying, there would be hell to pay for those in the path of his wrath. He began with Raul, the one between Chloe and the new boyfriend.

"I'mma start things off like this, because I wanna know who the fuck took out my cousin! They blew his brains out, then tossed him in the trash! My aunt-- Alfredo's mother--

not gonna rest or allow me to do so, until we get revenge. And I want blood **now** more than anything! How does it make me look in the streets if I don't do something about it! Like a weak piece of shit, that's what! I'm motherfuckin' *Tito Dominquez!* A Puerto Rican Don in Philly! I want all the smoke!" Tito barked vehemently in Spanish.

He had tears in his eyes and vengeance covering his heart, looking at each person fiercely who stood there with him.

"Raul and Enrique… Tell me straight up. Did y'all have anything to do with Chloe's new boyfriend being robbed for the product they had?" Tito emphatically asked.

The two looked at one another with guilty eyes and tattle-tale demeanors, trying to make a determination as to who would go first to spill the beans.

Enrique spoke up. "It was us, Tito. We did it."

"You were here with me that night. What you had to do with it?" Tito asked in response.

"I was the one who texted Alfredo and informed him when the two guys got here and left. Raul…" Enrique pointed out, "…was one of the people who blocked the men with the tow truck and took the car and all they had."

Tito took a look at Raul. "What you gotta say?"

"It's true. What he says is what happened. I ain't like that fucking nigga no way, Tito. I had to get back in good graces with my sweetheart, bro. You already know what Chloe means to me and I feel some type of way about those two being in a relationship," Raul admitted.

"So you're the main man behind this I see," said Tito.

"Alfredo was the one who really wanted to rob holmes for the weed and pills. He said he owed you and that would be a good way to get the money to pay you off," Raul said. "I only wanted to smack him around. That was it."

Tito thought over a few scenarios in his mind he now had. There was more reason to believe an act of retaliation was carried out by Von.

But if that was the case, why would he have his people intervene to pay back the debt he owed? And do Von even know who robbed him? Tito pondered.

"They don't know who y'all were, do they?" Tito asked both Enrique and Raul.

"Not that I know of," replied Raul. "And me and Chloe been seeing one another again lately. I think her and dude are on bad terms, he ain't been around too much."

"But I don't understand, Tito. How does that tie into Alfredo being killed and dumped in a landfill? Alfedo was my homie," stated Enrique.

"Mine too," Raul chimed in.

"And I don't care what. If you feel like the dude Von and them had anything to do with Alfredo's death, we should go at them. No ifs, ands, or buts about it, just hit 'em!" Enrique suggested.

"We just may do that. We just may. Let me find out a little more, then I'll tell y'all what we do from there. Hold tight until I give the word. And in the meantime, Raul, get Chloe to tell you all she knows about her boyfriend or whatever he is now," Tito stated.

"Not a problem, Tito. Not a problem at all, homie."

$$$$

Cold Heart, together with Lonnie and Kareem, added more hustlers to the ranks to help move the product they'd been increasing. Drip had Monk supply Cold Heart directly with ten kilos and kept Von and those who alternated with him, five at a time until he had a solid hold on Williamsport like he needed. In addition to the spot around Eric Ave and those takeovers in West Philly, they now had 24th and Somerset 12th and Huntingdon, Fairhill and York, and 25th and Masters. Every new location had some solid dude from the area now on the team. Progress was being made in a major way. And although the country was going through a recession, dopeheads still found a way to keep a few bucks in their pockets to get a heroin high with. Drip provided top-notch, high quality bricks at the time, only a few that the city had to offer.

One of Cold Heart's homies who ran the spot on 25th and Masters, a cat named Steve Northington aka "Fat Steve", came to him to present a problem brewing. Apparently, a dude named Brent Parker—who went by the street name of "Boss"—was attempting to put the press down and take over the drug corner, with his ten man crew..

"Yo Cold, we got a serious problem, bro," Fat Steve announced over the phone. *"Some fuck shit just happened."*

"Say no more. I'm on the way to you now. I'm not too far. At mom's house," Cold Heart responded, clearly now in anger.

He got in his car and made his way to the location.

Fat Steve sent a text message, letting him know he was posted outside the bodega three blocks way. Boss and his boys had robbed and pistol whipped Fat Steve and the two dudes he had with him. When Cold Heart arrived, Fat Steve got in the car and immediately began to relate the jack and beat down.

"Yo man, you got this nigga named Boss and a few of his homies, who just robbed us then smacked us down with their bangers!" he revealed.

He had a busted lip, swollen eye, and a couple knots dotted around the side of his head as proof of the assault.

"Word! So these niggas wanna be tough guys and gangstas, huh! We are about to handle that shit right now!" Cold Heart spat, then snatched his phone for the clip in his waistline to call someone.

The person on the other end answered.

"Yo, Heem! Suit up! I'm on the way to get you now," Cold Heart declared, then disconnect the call.

Faheem Coleman aka "Heem" was Cold Heart's younger cousin by one year and a young gunner for him as well.

Heem was the son of Cold Heart's uncle, the army veteran who'd taught him how to fight in military combat and how to properly shoot firearms.

"What the fuck them niggas take from y'all, bro?" Cold Heart asked.

"A few thousand in cash and like eight thousand in bundles," Fat Steve responded.

"Shit! Don't worry. We are about to handle that shit tonight. In a few minutes."

Cold Heart made it to Heem's spot on 67th and Organtz. He was suited and booted with the Desert Eagle pistol that Cold Heart had given to him.

"I'm ready to roll, fam," declared Heem.

"Good! Because we about to get some action in a few minutes," Cold Heart stated, then pulled out his pistol and cocked back the hammer with a round loaded into the chamber. He had a *Colt .45.*

They made it to the spot on 25th and Masters, passing through for Fat Steve to point out who Boss and his crew were.

"That's that nigga right there, Cold," said Steve.

"Heem, you see'm?"

"No doubt," Heem responded.

"I'mma let you out around the block. I want you to walk up to dude, act like you trynna cop baggies from him, then let that pussy have it! A'ight!"

"Check, fam."

Cold Heart let Heem out, then eased down the block to turn around.

"Don't nobody come and take SHIT from us, my nigga! You gotta handled your business without hesitation. This how we do! It's toe tags for niggas who get in the way of that money bag, homie ! Niggas gotta die when they violate any one of us! That's the code I live by!" Cold Heart spat. "By the way, where them other two niggas who was with you?"

"Them sucka-ass niggas ran off and left me by myself, Cold!"

"Enough said. They gonna get it too! Word to my dead twin sister, they are! And you and me gonna be the ones to pop them coward-ass niggas! How the fuck they gonna live to tell the story in a different way. Nah, dawg! Not on my watch! No how no way!" Cold Heart emphatically stated.

Fat Steve kept quiet and said nothing more.

Heem was approaching Boss at this point.

"What's good, what's good?!" Boss announced.

"We got them 'Death' baggies over here, homeboy. Twenty dollars a pop, B. How many you tryna cop?" he further said.

"Let me get like four of them shits, dawg," Heem responded. He had his hands on his four pound weighted *Desert Eagle* that was hidden inside the hoodie he had on.

"Four jawns coming up, my nigga. This shit so good, you sure you don't want five?" spoke Boss, looking to increase the amount in sales.

"As a matter of fact, yeah. Gimme five. Just be sure to add a zero at the end for *fifty caliber*, motherfucka!" spat Heem, already drawing down on dude by the time Boss had a chance to look up from the bundle he had his eyes on after hearing the comment behind Heem made.

"WHAT?!"

BANG!

The first blast was a headshot. A portion of Boss's skull was knocked off for from the powerful slug, causing him to collapse onto the pavement.

The three men that was with Boss ran into the house at that point.

BANG! BANG! BANG! BANG!

"There you go. Five of 'em you say, right?!" Heem spat. "Nigga, you got served!"

Heem then ran off down the block to meet back up with Cold Heart and Fat Steve, getting into the car, and they rode off.

The plan was to lay their heads down at the spot then return a few weeks later to resume activities.

$$$$$

One Day Later...

Cold Heart had Fat Steve to go by and pick up the two homies who was with him the night before, a somewhat chubby guy nicknamed "Meatball" and the other dude's name was Ill-Will, a slim hustler with height. He had about a six foot six inch frame.

Cold Heart had a low key spot in the Bad Lands areas of North Philly and he needed Steve to lure Meatball and Ill-Will there. The set up was that he wanted to talk with everybody to find out what all took place, do they possibly know who the cats were that Boss had with him, and to discuss the relocation to a new trap house to get money from that day onward.

Fat Steve arrived and had his so-called comrades in the car. They park and got out, entering the house. Steve was the last to come inside after closing and locking the door. Cold Heart was seated on the couch in the living room watching an NBA game. The locking of the dead bolt was the cue to take action.

POW!

Cold Heart sprung from his position and shot Ill-Will in the chest. He had his gun already locked and loaded underneath a pillow on the sofa next to him.

Ill-Will dropped to the floor.

POW!

Steve shot Meatball in the back of the head as he stood in a petrified state, watching as Cold Heart shot his partner.

Meatball's large body made a frightening thud sound upon slumping and hitting the carpeted floor.

BOOM!

Cold Heart shot Ill-Will in the face as he stood over him, wanting to be sure dude was dead. The first round wasn't good enough.

For Cold Heart, there honestly wasn't nothing to talk about. . He had nothing to say because the decision was already made when Fat Steve made him aware that the now two dead dudes had ran off on him.

"No hesitation, Steve. That's how we move and operate, my nigga! For any niggas who violate. Remember, it's toe tags for any motherfuckas who get in the way of the money." And that was that.

Chapter 16

In Williamsport...

Von, Ron, Khaddafi, and Khalil had two trap houses up and going and doing good numbers on the east side of the town in the heart of a hood there. Not too far down the block, about half football field, a few local cats who were born and raised there, had set up shop and were looking to get money as well. That presented a problem, and the Philly crew who'd planted their flag there, was now looking to check the situation because they for damn sure weren't going to repost it. The four of them approached to inquire about the issue.

"Yo, what up-what up?" Ron the elder of the four spoke up.

There were four Williamsport dudes posted on the porch. It was a Friday night around nine p.m.

"Who calling the shots over here?" Ron asked.

"I am, my nigga! Who wanna know?" responded the husky built and brolic dark-skinned cat as he got to his feet.

"I wanna know. Because I'm tryna find out who I directly need to speak my words to, for slowing up my paper down the block there," stated Ron.

"This block only big enough for *one* crew. And last I know, the strip belongs to *us*. The niggas who from 'round here. Born and raised in this town. Not from Philly," the Williamsport hustler spat, appearing fearless and maybe ready for whatever.

"I'm glad to know you aware of where we from. Maybe you did your homework. Maybe you hadn't. Who's to say? And just so you know, it ain't where you from. It ain't where you are. It's *who* you are. And how long you been out here doing your thing, my guy?" Ron continued on.

"Look, my nigga. I been out here all my life. This is *my* hood. My mom and people live right down the block there. I got the right to get money out here how I feel. Me and my niggas right here," dude grimaced and gestured with a wave of his hand at his homies.

"Yo, we ain't got no problem with you getting money. You just can't get money out here. On **this** block. You understand?!" Ron spat.

"Nah, nigga! You got that backwards. We ain't got no problem with *y'all* getting money. Y'all just can't do so here on **our** block! And I'm Pac-Man to you, homie. You walking up like you know something more, dude. This *my* spot... it was five years ago when I was out here, and it is now, since I'm out again, ya dig!" Pac-Man stated emphatically.

"You say Pac-Man, huh?"

"Pac-Mac, my nigga. A Williamsport OG."

"Five years ago, where were you, Pac-Man?"

"Five years ago, I had just got locked up."

"You say you were born and raised here?"

"Born and raised, my nigga. My Momma here, my Poppa here, everyone here. My whole family from Williamsport, and ain't no outta town niggas gonna pull-up in my town and tryna tell me what the fuck to do!"

"So what the fuck you sayin', nigga!" spat Ron.

"What the fuck you mean, *what the fuck I'm sayin'?!* What the fuck *you* sayin'!" Pac-Man retorted with a lot of aggression.

"This what the fuck I'm saying, nigga!!"

POW!

Von was the one who'd let off the first shot, hitting Pac-Man in the chest.

Everyone on both sides immediately pulled out their guns and began blasting at one another. Ron and crew backed away, shooting and trying to take position behind cars that filled the one way strip while Pac-Man's crew scurried towards the front door of the house.

Pac-Man was holding his chest and down on one hand and both knees, attempting to crawl for the porch.

Khaddafi took notice of the wounded victim.

I'm 'bout to murk that pussy! he thought to himself.

An intense moment took place where both crews exchanged a vicious volley of gunfire at one another. Then, a pause occurred. Khaddafi jumped to the occasion.

He ran up to Pac-Man, stood over him from behind, then began blasting.

BANG-BANG-BANG-BANG-BANG!

He shot dude five times in rapid succession, once in the back of the head, and four rounds to the back.

They all sprinted quickly down the block jumped into the car that they had and made their way to the farm house just on the outskirts of the city. The plan was for Ron and the twins to head back to Philly the next day until the heat was no more. And Von had to stay put for all the reasons he had.

Of the four with Pac-Man and his crew, him and another guy died. The remaining ones couldn't identify no one. All that was needed from that point was for Von's guys to relocate and establish themselves on the opposite side of town. An available option they already had in mind to do.

The following day, Von took a trip back home to Philly. He needed to at least check-in on his grandmother, Chloe, Monyetta, Rosa, and his sister, Kidada. He was in a rented gray Dodge Magnum. Dude loved that style of cars. He went by to see Nana fist. She was so happy so see him. They hug tightly.

"Vonnie! Baby, granny's happy to see you," Mrs. Edna expressed. Her eyes welled in tears from emotion.

"I'm happy to see you too, Nana. And I love you," Von responded.

"And now we've got to get your Momma out of that place. She don't sound too worried when she calls. And when that girlfriend of your takes me to see her. She don't look bothered either. But I am," said Mrs. Edna.

"Me too, Nana. I promise you. She'll be out soon. We've gotta continue to be patient, that's all," Von responded, then took a tour around house, being sure Monyetta helped Mrs. Edna straightened out the mess the police made in their search.

"I like that pretty girlfriend of yours too, Vonnie. She's smart as well. Say she's in college. And before long, I may see her on the Channel Nine News."

Von smiled at the comments made by his grandmother. He spent another half hour with Mrs. Edna, provided her the new phone number he had, then left en route to see his chocolate cutie, Monyetta.

When he pulled into her apartment complex, her *Jeep Cherokee* was in the parking space. Von still had a key to her place. He texted on the ride from Williamsport to let her know he'd be there.

Von exited the rental, approached the apartment door, then let himself in. The time was just past eight p.m. She were showering.

"Monyetta! It's me boo! Where you at?" he called out for her.

"I'm in the shower, sweetheart. About to come out now," Monyetta responded.

Von then heard the water running and made his way to the bathroom to peep his head through the door, both of them laying eyes on one another. He smiled at the sight of her and her naked body. She had the glass shower door half opened for him to see. Water beads were dotted all over her body.

"Hey, baby" Von let out sensuously, smiling.

"Hey, sweetheart. How you been?" Monyetta responded with a smile.

Von stepped into the bathroom. "I've been good. Missed you like crazy and was ready to see you," he said. "Here I am."

"Yes you are," she replied with a loving smile, beautiful white teeth on display.

"Come on. I want you to join me. You look like you need a hot shower and a good body massage," Monyetta let out further.

Von began to strip down out of his clothes in preparation to enter the shower. Monyetta adjusted the hot water temperature to a degree lower so Von could tolerate it. She loved the water to be as hot as it could be to keep her skin soft and tender. He stepped inside. Von's compassionate and caring companion then lathered the soap sponge and began to bathe him.

Once they'd gotten done washing up, the two made their way to the bedroom to continue what they'd started.

Monyetta had a jar of fragrant massage oil she love to lubricate with. She made way to the kitchen to heat the oil in the microwave. She returned to the bedroom to find Von stretched out on the bed and ready to be caressed by his sensational sweetheart. Of all the females he had in his life, he was really falling for Monyetta like no other. She moved him in a special way.

Following an intense session of body massages and good sex, the two laid in the nude and fell asleep tightly hugged up.

The next morning, Von hit Cold Heart up to see how he were doing. He had his homie swing by Monyetta's place so they could talk and catch up on a few things. Von also had Monyetta to get in touch with her sister, Tiona, so that her and Cold Heart may finally have the opportunity to meet one another and get acquainted. Cold Heart was there at eleven a.m. Tiona was intent on being there soon.

Von let Cold Heart inside.

"What's good, bro," stated Von as he and his homie dapped one another then hug in embrace.

"I'm good, homie. Happy to see you. Been thinking about our years as friends and growing up and shit. You already know I love to think over the past and reminisce on a lot of things," Cold Heart responded.

He and Von then took a seat in the living room.

"Whose crib is this?" Cold Heart asked.

"Oh, this one of the shorty's crib. I deal with Monyetta. You ain't never met her before?"

"Nah. You only gave her name before. The college chick, right?"

"Yeah, her," Von confirmed. "Monyetta!" he called out.

She appeared from the back, dressed in pajamas.

"Yeah, sweetie?" she responded.

"Hey, this my homie here, Eunice. We've been cool since childhood. He's like the brother I never had. I need for you to treat him and respect him in that way, okay?" Von stated in a serious tone.

"Okay, baby. Hey, Eunice. How are you?" Monyetta looked over at Cold Heart and greeted.

"I'm good. And it's nice to meet you…Monyetta."

There was a very specific reason why Von gave Monyetta Cold Heart's real name and not the street name he now went by. He wanted her to get familiar with him as the person and friend he knew because with the future ahead of him, she would definitely be seeing him more often. And also, if anything was to go wrong with Von, Monyetta would have to contact Cold Heart, in addition to knowing how to get in touch with Von's cousin, Monk. He and her best friend, Ayonna, were still in a relationship.

The two homies went on to relate the things they'd done while apart, including the people they'd kill and the progress or lack thereof made in the streets. Von then let Cold Heart know he would have a female visitor shortly. A cutie like Monyetta.

"I hooked you up with a sweetheart, bro. Since I ain't never but a few times seen your ugly ass with a female," Von joked.

"Fuck you, Von. I don't know what make you think I don't get any pussy. I do. *A lot* of it if you must know. I don't go for those high maintenance chicks like you, Drip, and Monk. I prefer hood bitches, bro. Them less fortunate females of the struggle, you know. To be honest, they are the ones who gonna ride it out with you in the worst of times. They'll never be the ones to let you down. And they don't forget about times you came through for them or when they needed you most and you delivered. You feel me," Cold Heart expressed.

"I do. And to tell you the truth, I never thought I'd be able to get you to speak on the subject of females like that. You took me by surprise. But nonetheless, Monyetta's sister's name is Tiona. Tiona Laurens," stated Von.

"She nice too, bro," Von added as he raised his eyebrows for emphasis while looking on at his homie.

They both smiled to indicate the understanding of Tiona being a sexy female Cold Heart could grow to love and appreciate.

A couple hours later, Tiona appeared. Throughout the time between, Von and Cold Heart entertained themselves playing *Madden NFL* on the PlayStation Monyetta bought for him as a gift.

Tiona were just as lovely and had sex appeal like her younger sibling. Only slightly taller.

The four of them made it a fun day out together at *Dave and Busters*. Cold Heart and Tiona hit it off well. Their chemistry was amazing, expressing a good girl who fell for a bad boy type vibe.

Although Tiona hailed from an upper middle class family and grew up in an affluent neighborhood in Upper Darby, Pennsylvania, without having to say it, she was willing to compromise and be that diehard loyal 'hood chick; Cold Heart was all too familiar with. Tiona adored his grungy and tough appearance he possessed, aligned with the rough around the edges and lack of grooming and the mentality that accompanied Cold Heart. She'd hid it long enough. A hardcover thug nigga was what she wanted, and Cold Heart was nowhere near short in being the gangster Tiona long dreamed of having. A match in heaven made by Von.

Chapter 17

Drip was on campus at the Ivy League School of Penn University there in Philly. He had two reasons for being there. One was because his young sweetheart, the beautiful and very sexy Divida Naomi Anderson, asked him to be there to show support for her and the volleyball team she was apart of. And to also have a business meeting and discussion with his primary heroin supplier, Jack Xiaoping. Jack's daughter attended the school as well.

Drip appeared thirty minutes before the first serve of the game. Divida had just dressed out into her uniform, displaying her nice plump round ass. Those tight fitting performance shorts and top magnified the level of sex appeal she had along with her feminine grace that was highly displayed.

"Vida!" Drip called out to her, making her aware of his presence and for her to approach him for a moment. She did so.

"Hey, Damien," greeted the five foot six inch brown skinned and fit sweetheart.

"Hey, babe," he responded.

The two then kissed. Drip strode his hand over her enticing ass cheeks while complementing the touch, and maintaining eye contact along with their smiles.

"I'm glad you took the time this afternoon from your busy day to come support me and my girls," Divida said.

"Anything for you, baby. You're my future. And I've got a lot of love for you," Drip expressed sincerely.

"Aw! That's so sweet of you. It really is."

They then kissed once more.

"I'mma be right here, all right."

"Perfect. Then after my game, we can go out to eat. You know I love *Applebees.* And we can't forget about the school donation that need to be made," said Divida.

"You know I'm on top of it, babe. And I've got to meet with your business major friend's father, Jack. We've got a few property developments to discuss."

"Understood. I'll be back shortly, okay. And I like that outfit. All Gucci everything. Dope," complimented Divida with a smile, as she backpaddled in steps then turn to go warm up with the team.

Drip had on a velour sweatsuit with the hat, sneakers, watch, and eyeglass frames to match. Everything was as Divida stated they were…All *Gucci* everything. Dude was a high profile, high class dope boy fresh. *That* nigga indeed!

Not too much longer, the game began. Divida's team played Princeton. The score was seven to five, Penn leading the first set. Jack entered around that time. Drip was seated in his usual spot on the bottom row near the entrance section. Jack layed eyes on him. The two then made their way to the very top of the bleachers out of earshot of everyone else as they always had each time they'd met there. Sporting events were always occuring there in the gym.

Drip opened up to begin the talks. "It's a pleasure to have you meet me yet again, Jack. I'm always grateful to be in business with you."

"My pleasure to be here, Damien. I'm always motivated by money and the prospect of continuing doing business with you. You're one of my valued clients. I appreciate you and your ambition," responded the calm clean shaven first generation forty-two year old Chinese-American.

"As you already know, this recession we're going though currently, has hampered the both of us in a way. And although the product I buy from you is moving but not at the pace I'm used to. Items have changed, Jack, and so has the way people like to get high. For us to keep up and stay ahead of the wave, we've got to diversify and create various other products to accommodate the dealers and users," Drip stated.

Jack gazed at him and smiled. His Asian features were on full display, small tight lips, tea stained teeth, slitted eyes, and stretched skin of the face.

"I like the way you think, Damien. You're a very smart twenty-eight year old guy. The more we discuss and do business, the more I come to the conclusion that I made a good choice when I added you to my elite list of clients. My product doesn't go to any and everyone who profess to be dealers. Only those who have vision and are able to see the future deserve my blessings. With that been said, let me make you aware of the things I've done. Me and the network I'm apart of, have created and designed various pills that are becoming increasingly popular with the original product. Also, a now more powerful type of material is making its way into the market. It's called *Fentanyl*. We use it to add to the heroin and press the pills with it included… with the objective to make the pills more suitable for the party scene. And all the products are highly addictive and greatly desired."

Jack provided an extensive monologue.

"I see you're already atop of this. Now only thing left to discuss is the price of the pills, and whether or not the price for the kilos I already buy from you will increase or decrease," stated Drip.

"You already know I'm a fair man, Damien. I won't alter the current price we already have in place. So long as you don't spend less than the four million each order as you do."

"I won't. In fact, I'll spend five this time. Now what about those pills?" Drip inquired.

"My plan is to lay two million worth on you on consignment, to get you going properly. We'll worry about you paying for it later down the line. Is that okay?" asked Jack.

"Absolutely. I can't beat that."

"And are you prepared to be re-supplied?"

The two made eye contact and shook hands to secure the deal.

Drip drove the Range Rover that day. He had the five million in cash stowed away inside until the game ended. His plan was to use one of his credit cards to make a $5,000 donation for Divida. Drip had no problem waiting until the next day to be provided the product he purchased and would be fronted. He and Body would have his transporter pick up and deliver with them trailing. Of course, the transporter was Body's brother, Pervis, a police lieutenant.

The volleyball game ended, Divida showered, dressed, and was ready to go out to eat. She, Drip, Jack, and Jack's daughter, Amy, all exited the gym of the university. Amy supported her classmate and friend by attending the game and having her father also make a donation.

Jack had his driver pull closely to the S.U.V. that Drip drove to make the exchange. They then drove off, leaving Drip and Divida in peace to go on about their night. The two made their way to the *Applebees* on Old York Road. Their night concluded well.

$$$$$

Von was still around Philly for a time being and lying low from one spot to another. From Monyetta's place to checking in on his grandma Rosa's apartment and to the house he and Chloe had together. He stayed clear of Cori's house. It was too deep in the hood. Also, he didn't want her to know he was in town. Von didn't want to explain to four different females and give four different versions as to why he was there and why he wouldn't be able to spend all of his time with them individually. He had plans to keep still three to four weeks, then return to Williamsport. The heat should be down by then.

While at he and Chloe's place, she made him aware of a few things.

"Von, I don't know what the problem is, but my cousin Tito had a lot of questions about you. Like, *a lot* of questions, sweetie. I thought y'all worked out the situation already?" She wanted to know.

"We did. I wonder why the hell he is still going on about that. Me and my people worked that out."

"He seem to want to know about any business you may had going on with our cousin, Alfredo."

"Alfredo?! I never had any business with him."

"And I told him that. But to be honest, he seem to be trying to get down to the bottom of who killed him?"

"How the fuck would I know?"

"He asked did you mention anything about who you thought robbed you. I told him you hadn't. That you just left it alone."

My homie Cold Heart was right all along. That nigga Tito had to tell them motherfuckas to rob us. Snake-ass nigga! Now he was feeling sorry because his people got put down. We need to hit his ass! He and the other nigga who had something to do with it, Von thought himself.

"That's what I'd done. Just left it alone. But anyway, did those cops take anything when they raided?"

"Nah. They just tore the place up," Chloe related then got to her feet from the bed, walked over to the dresser, and retrieved the copy of the search warrant to show Von.

Von began to read it. "What the fuck! These motherfuckas crazy!" he let out.

The wording of the warrant hit a panic button in Von. He'd begun to feel vulnerable in a way, moving erratically and preparing to leave.

"What's wrong, Vonnie?" Chloe asked.

"I gotta get outta here, baby! And I want you to be busy tomorrow looking for another place to stay. Aight. Tomorrow, Chloe. We not safe here anymore. Ain't no telling when they may want to come back. I'm glad neither one of us was here when they kicked in the door."

"I'll do that. And we need to do everything we can to bring your trouble with the cops to an end, Vonnie. I'm getting afraid. I need you back close to me now more than anything. More than *anything,* Vonnie," she reiterated, "because I can't do this by myself any longer," she let out with a shudder to her voice and a tear in her eye.

"What's going on with you, Chloe? You can't do *what* by yourself?"

"Raise a baby, Von. I'm pregnant," she revealed. "I'm pregnant with our baby. I took a test last week when my period didn't come. And that's why I say we've got to get your situation worked out with the police, so we can focus on our baby."

Von smiled excitedly at the news he'd just been provided.

"For real, Chloe. I'm about to be a father?"

"Yes, Von…Yes you are. We've got *a baby* on the way. And we need to get busy prioritizing a reality for our baby. While we're ahead and are able. Understand?"

"I do. And we're gonna make it right, long before the baby gets here. Okay," Von said.

They hugged and kissed.

"Okay, baby. That's what we're gonna do," Chloe responded.

"Now I've got to get outta here. Call me when you feel the need to. And I love you, Chloe. Never forget that."

"I love you too, Trevon. Don't you forget that."

"And be sure to call me on three-way when my mom calls you. Okay."

"I will."

Von left out the house and made his way to go see Rosa. She'd texted him a few times throughout the day.

$$$$$

Upon arriving at Rosa's apartment, he made his way to the door and was met by her. She was happy to see him and a bit of concern was dashed on her face as well.

He stepped inside and Rosa closed the door before they hugged and kissed. While looking into her eyes, Von had the thought pass through his mind of everything Chloe shared with him and all Rosa had said to him about Chloe.

Should I tell her? Or should I not? he pondered to himself.

"What's good? What's on your mind?" he asked.

"Been missing you like crazy. Haven't seen you in a few weeks. And now I've got my feelings caught up in you, I want to see you every day. I like what we have started, Von. How do you feel about me? What do we have?"

"I really don't know how to tell you. If you want me to be honest, I like what we have. But what do we do with what we have?" Von expressed himself.

"We need to do more fun things together like we've been doing. Then move into business together. And hopefully, in due time, we'll be able to live out aloud what we have in the dark. Out in the open. Once what you and Chloe have no longer exist," Rosa stated emphatically.

Von took a hard look at Rosa. She patiently waited to hear what he had on his mind to say.

"I don't think that'll be happening any time soon," he let out.

"You don't think what'll be happening no time soon?" Rosa asked.

"Me and Chloe being completely done with one another."

She starred at him before making a comment.

"Why you say that?" Rosa had to ask.

Von felt no need to hold back with what he had to say.

"Because she's pregnant. She told me today."

Rosa didn't appear to be fazed by the revelation, but she did feel the need to push back in a way.

"She's *pregnant!* By who? Does she know?" Rosa remarked sarcastically.

"Don't forget *I'm* the one who told you the truth about all she has goin' on. But I don't want to go on about that. I'm not a hater. I'm a participant, baby. And you've got a job to do with me now. It's *my* turn. So come on. Let's get busy making *our* baby," Rosa let out, then started getting naked right there in the living room, dropping to the floor for a quickie.

"I want you to fuck me, Von. Right here, right now," Rosa demanded in a sexually aggressive tone.

Von loved when Rosa talked to him in that way. His dick got hard instantly. It took him little to no time at all to get out of the *Adidas* nylon sweat suit he was wearing. Rosa already had his manhood in her mouth as he was taking off his jacket and tee shirt.

She pulled on him with passion and relentlessness until he were fully erect. Rosa then layed on her back atop of the carpeted floor. Von straddled her, penetrated her wet entrance, and began to work in the way she loved him to. They fucked like crazy and really had a good time. She'd made an impression on him that night. One that she could cash in on later down the line.

Chapter 18

At The Police Department...

Everything J-Dubb related to the police of his whereabouts the evening of the shooting of Feezy and Dedra had checked out. The video surveillance of the motel he and the female acquaintance reserved showed the couple there hours before the street camera captured his car fleeing the scene. Also, motel surveillance of the parking lot revealed that the entire time J-Dubb and Tina were there, the Ford Taurus wasn't. Therefore, they had no choice but to release J-Dubb and drop all the charges. Bill used his last play in his bag of tricks before setting the accused back on the street.

Bill used J-Dubb's cell phone to send a text message to the contact "Baby Girl" to see what type of reply he'd get. Valco was there at his desk and by his side to offer assistance. The first text was sent:

J-DUBB's PHONE: Baby girl. Hey. It's me.

Shayla was taken totally by surprise by the message that she received on her end of the phone.

What the fuck!

SHAYLA: J-Dubb! Where the fuck you at? Where have you been? Why the fuck me and Tangee ain't heard from you in two months? And call me right now!

"Valco, we've got some serious action here." Bill made his sidekick aware.

Valco leaned in to have a look at the message.

"I'm lost on how to reply," stated Bill.

"Let me have at it, Bill," Valco insisted.

Bill handed him the device.

J-DUBB'S PHONE: "You ain't heard from me because I'm in rehab trying to get my life together. I knew I had to contact you to let you know I'm ok. And I can't call. We really are not allowed phones here at the center.

SHAYLA: Oh Ok. I understand. Hope all is well with you. And I'm praying for you too, Dubbs.

J-DUBB'S PHONE: Thanks. But hey, Baby girl, I gotta ask. Where were you in my car the last time I let you use it? One of my people I get high with said something to me about seeing my car leaving fast on Cecil B. Moore, some dude and kid got shot.

Valco made it his business to get straight to the point in the text message exchange. He knew the right questions to ask.

SHAYLA: Oh that. It wasn't nothing. Me and my boyfriend had an argument and I sped off over in the area. I don't know anything about a shooting though.

"Hey Bill, we really got something here. This 'Baby Girl' female just admitted to being in the Cecil B. Moore area the evening of the shooting."

Bill took a closer look and re-read the text. "See can you get more out of her. Maybe mention the name of the guy who was shot."

"*Feezy* is the nickname of his that Davis provided, right?" stated Valco.

"That's right. Esha Davis. The mother of the little girl killed."

"Mmm-hmm!"

J-DUBB'S PHONE: How about that boyfriend of yours. Feezy stopped me one day when I went to your place to see you. This was a day or two after Christmas. I didn't see you any more after that. Where did you go?

SHAYLA: How do you know his name, J-Dubb?

"We've got a connection, Bill. Richardson and this Baby Girl."

"Shayla Allen's her name. Phone record and email reveal," responded Bill.

"She wants to know how Washington is aware of Richardson's nickname," related Valco.

"She's Washington's dealer. She mentioned it to him before," Bill advised him to relate.

J-DUBBS PHONE: You mentioned it to me before. Remember?

SHAYLA: I may have. I don't remember. But anyway, we broke up and he won't be around any longer to speak of. That bitch ass nigga out of my life. Forever!

"Would you look at this shit!" Valco let out. "We may have a confession here about same things, Bill."

"Quiz her more about that 'forever' part, if you will. And try to find out why she seems to hate Richardson the way she does."

"Gotcha"

J-DUBB'S PHONE: What do you mean by "Forever?" And why do you seem to hate him? You two were just in love. And he said something to me that day I came to your place about him and his daughter being shot. That he believes you know something about it. Keep it real with me Baby Girl.

SHAYLA: Like I said Dubbs. That bitch-ass nigga out my life. Forever! Fuck him and his daughter too! I don't give a fuck if she dead or not! And I gotta go. We can text more some other time. You take care. And I'm happy for you.

"Well I be damned!" exclaimed Bill.

"I know right. We can't get a confession any better than this, can we?"

"No we can't. All we've got to do now is identify who she is and go get a warrant to bring her in," said Bill.

"Let's get busy doing that," replied Valco.

"Let's do that, shall we?" said Bill.

The two then made preparations to pursue Shayla in arrest.

$$\$\$\$\$\$$$

Drip retained Levi as the lawyer to represent Von's mother, Lilly, and had him do all necessary to get her free. Drip knew the whole story and was aware that the cops wanted Von more so than they did Lilly. The objective was to get Lilly free first, have her and Von meet with him and Levi together, and do all that Levi suggested needed to be done to dispose of the case, then they could move on about their lives.

Also, Von's father, Little Hound, was on the verge of being freed in the coming months and he knew that the father would want to at least spend time with his son in the free world. In the end Levi would need Von to turn himself in to police to resolve the mess.

Little Hound called Drip on video. The two had a conversation.

"Drip, how you been, fam? I'm glad to have this opportunity to see you and talk to you," said Hound Jr.

"No doubt, fam. Always a pleasure. I can't wait until you're free and back out here. We're gonna do it really big this go around. I'm up in a major way now J-R," Drip boosted.

"Making power moves like no other," stated Drip.

"For sho', fam. That's what we Savages do, you know. My pop and your grandpa laid the foundation and showed us the way. We can't do anything but succeed. I always believed in you, Drip. Even though you're six years younger than me and didn't have too much experience in the street like I had, you made it through the storm. And I'm proud of you, fam. I'm ready for us to get back to doing what we do. How your little bro, Monk, doing? He and Vonnie locked in and making it?" Little Hound asked.

"Yeah, they're good. Ever since the day you told me to have Monk get in touch with Vonnie and bring him on in with what we got going, he's been making progress."

"Yeah man, his mom let me know he was out there in those streets and trying to hustle. And if that was the decision he'd made, no one would be able to turn him in a different direction. So we may as well lead him in the right way and who better than me, to teach him how to hustle other than you? Since the both of us use to get money in a family connected way. Right?"

"Right, fam. And not only that, how about Vonnie was already commanding a mean little crew when I put him down with me?" Drip related.

"Word!"

"Word! Them little niggas was getting it too. They sold a different product though. But I got them all pumping our product of choice. And not only that, Vonnie got a homie he grew up with, who puts in the *other* work. Real good at it too," Drip stated, then agitated his trigger finger to indicate shooter.

"I wonder who groomed him?" Hound Jr asked.

"He said something about having an uncle who was in the military. Young boul like that, fam. I've already put him to the test. I paired him up with my homie, Body. He checked all the boxes. I had no choice but to bring him in closer to me."

"I know he's gotta be official if you got him part of your inner circle."

"Hell yeah he is. But anyway. On another note. Lilly should be up for a bail hearing in the next couple of weeks. They still holding her while they looking for Vonnie. The best part about that is, they don't even know what lil fam look like," Drip revealed to Von's father.

"Oh they don't?"

"Nope. Not at all. And I hooked him up with a new identity already. He not around the city any more either."

"Where he go?"

"I had him and his homies go up to Williamsport and plant our flag there. Vonnie really know what he doing, fam. He's really street smart. I had to salute him. Little fam and his crew up to fifteen units of H so far. Them young niggas moving that dope I tell you," Drip complimented.

"Goddamn! They doing it like that even in the recession!"

"The niggas doing like that even in the recession, fam! They got spots in north, spots out west, and the one upstate in Williamsport," related Drip.

"Damn! They are making moves huh. I'mma have to find a way to keep up with that nigga when I get out, I see."

"You damn sure are. But anyway, look. Hit me back this weekend, fam. I just hit A-C. I'm about to enjoy myself these next two days. Me and a sweetheart of mine," Drip said then turned the phone mounted on the cup console in the direction of Divida. She and him were on date night on a Thursday.

"Hello!" Divida greeted Little Hound with a warm smile and a waving of the hand.

"Hey! How are you?" Hound Jr. responded.

"I'm good. Nice to meet you."

"Nice to meet you too."

"Aight, fam. I'm out. Be easy. One love! Savage love!" Drip lastly said.

"One love. Savage love."

The call came to an end.

Drip and the Young Ivy League sensation were riding in his Range Rover. They'd made it to the city limits of Atlantic City on the expressway. The beautiful colorful lights illuminated the gambling haven and held a magical effect over the betting oasis. The two were intent on having a good time together. They were really into one another. Who's to say how far they had the potential to go. The sky's the limit.

PART THREE

Chapter 19

Two Months Later...

After a prolonged legal battle back and forth to the court to push for her bail to be granted and to reduce it, Lillian Dietrich, the strong vigilant and determined mother of Von, finally had the opportunity to post bond at amount of $1,000,000 (ten percent to the bondsman). Von put up half and Drip the other. She'd been free three weeks now and resumed living her life the way she had prior to the arrest. Lilly was allowed the chance to go back to work at the airport for American Airlines, as her now lawyer, Levi Jacobson, argued on her behalf that the charges she faced would no doubt be dropped. If not, there would be no job. The content of those words sounded far better coming from a high profile Jewish attorney than it would have coming from Lillian herself. The employer's board concluded to allow her to return.

On her first day free, she and her son met up at the new location where Von and Chloe now lived. They had an apartment in Bensalem, Pennsylvania, a popular suburb of Philadelphia. Only 15 to 20 minutes to the north, up I-95. Lilly had not had the opportunity to see her son in months. She was so happy to see him that day.

"Vonnie! Baby! Mommy loves you and missed you, son! I really did!" Lilly expressed then hugged Von tightly and kissed him like she'd just gave birth to him all over again.

"I missed you too, Mom, and I love you as well," Von responded.

The mother and son went to the back room to have a conversation over the incident and Von's warrant situation. Chloe remained in the kitchen cooking a meal.

"Vonnie, I didn't tell them shit, son! Nothing at all! You hear me! Nothing!"

"I know, mom. Kiki and that lawyer Drip got for you kept us informed about everything. From what I know, they don't even know how I look."

"Right! Because you don't have a license to drive. And you don't have a record. But at some point, baby, we're gonna have to do something to make this whole thing go away. But we'll cross that bridge when we get there. Right now, I'm just blessed to be free and relieved to know you're safe. That's all momma concerned about."

"Yeah, I'm good, ma. I have been keeping out of the way to the best of my ability. But anyway, grandma good? I ain't had a chance to go by to see her in a few days. Maybe a week. I called and talked to her though. This your first day home and I'm sure you've stopped by already, right?"

"I stopped by there before I came here. Momma's okay. She said something about you having some pretty little girlfriend of yours checking on her every other day. I thought she was talking about Chloe but then I remembered the other one you got that paid me a visit that one time. The dark skinned one, what's her name?"

"Monyetta, mom," Von answered, "and she was the one had taking care of Nana."

Lilly looked at him and smiled pleasantly. She then shook her head slowly.

"It must be nice, son. Must be nice, I tell you. Two pretty young ladies who are crazy about you."

Von returned a smile himself. "It is nice, mom. And me and Chloe expecting too," he announced to Lilly.

"For real, baby?!" Lilly let out ecstatically. "I've got a grandchild on the way?"

"Yes, ma'am, you do. She's about two months pregnant now. Almost three."

"I thought I noticed those hips of hers spread some," Lilly humored.

Lilly then opened the room door and made her way to the kitchen, smiling at Chloe.

"Chloe! Congratulations boo-boo! Vonnie told me you've got a bun in the oven, baby. I'm so happy for you two," Lilly said, then hugged Chloe and kissed her dearly on the cheekbone.

"Yep. We've got a little one on the way," responded Chloe. "I'm gonna be a mother, Miss Lilly."

"I can't wait either. We're gonna spoil my grandbaby rotten."

"Now that…we're definitely gonna do."

Lilly and Chloe hugged once more. She then returned to the bedroom to resume talking with her son.

"Mom, who's Jamar? Nana told me you had him come by a few times to check in on her. And the lawyer Drip got for you mentioned his name a time or so. Levi said he's part of the reason why the blame wasn't all out on you. That you and Jamar had been together all that day."

"Jamar is my new boyfriend, Von. I had left Bernard alone so I could be with him. He's nice to me. Jamar stayed by me throughout this entire ordeal. And I do have plans to introduce the two of you someday soon."

"That's good to know. But in the meantime, what the lawyer talking about?" Von asked.

"He told me we won't know nothing until we get a *'Discovery'* from the DA. And that won't occur until after the indictment. But from what he knows, they want you to turn yourself in."

"Ain't no way that's gonna happen, ma! No way!" Von vehemently protested.

Lilly shook her head from left to right, unsure of exactly what to say to her son to best advise him on which route they could take as the case played itself out.

"They don't necessarily have anything on me, son. The detective, some fat, black, and ugly grizzly bear looking motherfucka told me out his own mouth that they know I didn't pull the trigger. But thought I lured Bernard to the house and had you shoot him. That shit is so far from the truth. You and I know what really happened in that house. And had you not been there, I may be dead and not be here to talk to you. I'm more than sure everything is gonna be okay," Lilly said then gave her son another hug and kissed him on the forehead.

The three of them ate the meal Chloe made and spent the rest of the evening together. Later on, Von had gotten a text and a phone call from someone who was important in his life. They wanted to talk and share time with him. The person made him aware that there was an urgent issue they needed to discuss. One good, one not so good. It was Rosa, so Von made his way over to see her.

$$$$$

J-Dubb was let free from lock-up and had the urge to go out and get high. He'd gotten his car back from the police once they'd searched it for a weapon and possibly any other evidence that may had been there. None were discovered. The detectives had no choice but to release the car from the impound.

J-Dubb was out riding in his car and was near the area and the house where Shayla and Tangee lived and hustled. He decided to ride through the block in the hopes that he'd have the chance to lay eyes on "Baby Girl" and have her bless him with a few baggies until he would be able to pay her later down the line.

J-Dubb was under the impression that the girl may be still at the motel in New Jersey. But he knew it wouldn't take *that* long for the house to be "remodeled," the lie Shayla told to him the day they'd taken refuge across the bridge.

Upon pulling up in front of the house, he was taken by surprise to see Shayla and Tangee seated on the stoop doing what they do. It was early April and the weather was warm that afternoon. They recognized his car and him behind the wheel. He parked and got out to talk with them.

"Dubbs! What up, homie! How you been, my guy? We missed you," Shayla expressed.

"Shit, I been good. Couldn't wait to get the fuck up outta that damn place, I'm ready to get high now, Baby girl. Y'all holding?"

"Damn Dubbs! I thought you cleaned yourself up, my nigga! Rehab was that bad?" asked Shayla.

"Rehab?!" he retorted. "Hell you get that from?"

"From *you*. You texted me that night, remember?"

"I've been *in jail*, Baby Girl. And I ain't texted you since the day I took y'all to Jersey. Or picked you up from Jersey that day and dropped you off in West Philly. The cops pulled me over and locked my black ass up that same day! Talking about they had my car on a street camera fleeing the scene of a shooting. Some dude and a kid got shot! I don't know shit about that!" explained J-Dubb.

"What?! You didn't text me not too long the day before?"
"Nah! I couldn't. The two detectives had my phone. They never gave it back."

Shayla took her phone from her purse and showed J-Dubb the messages she'd received.

"Baby Girl, I didn't send those," he said convincingly.

She had an appalling look on her face. Shayla then made it her business to call the number to see if anyone would answer but the phone was no longer in service.

The thought of Feezy passed through her mind and she knew he was a goner and wouldn't be coming back. She was the one who'd put not one, not two, but *three* pieces of lead in his skull, thanks to Cold Heart. And if an investigation was going on, it definitely died with the death of Feezy. No doubt about it in Shayla's mind.

"Well whatever the situation was, Dubbs, that shit over and done with, my nigga. **Completely!**"

"I hear that. I damn sure do. I believe them no good bastards was trying to frame me for something. Once my story checked out about where I was around the time they claimed my car was caught on camera, they let me go without any problems. My momma let me know too that they'd came by the house a couple of times," he said. "But anyway, fuck all that! I'm tryna get high! Right now, you heard me."

J-Dubb had a funny way of expressing himself when he wanted a fix of heroin, causing the two girls to giggle and laugh like crazy.

"And I ain't got no money right now either. So you gonna have to spot me, Baby Girl," J-Dubb said.

"I gotcha, Dubb. And we got a car now, so I won't be borrowing yours anymore. Thank you for the time you did let me hold yours though," Shayla responded.

"Baby girl, hit me off with some dope will you! I'm geeking like crazy now!"

The girls laughed again. Shayla then dug into her purse and withdrew a $100 bundle of the product she sold and passed it to J-Dubb.

"Thank you, Baby Girl. Now y'all two give me a hug so I can go."

He did a *shimmy* dance, hugged Shayla and Tangee, then hurry and got into his car and rode off, en route to a nearby shooting gallery he knew about. The two girls continued to chill and handle their business on the block. They didn't know what to make of the news J-Dubb related about the cops having his phone. They knew he wasn't lying. But being that Feezy was a dead man, there was nothing to fear, or so Shayla thought.

$$$$$

Von made it to Rosa's house the day she'd called for him to do so. She had a smile on her face and a level of energy he'd never seen in her before. Upon entering the house, Rosa immediately hug him and they began to tongue kiss.

"What you so happy about, sweetheart?" he asked.

"I'm happy because you gave me a good reason to be this way. And I want to thank you for giving me *exactly* what I asked of you," she responded.

He chuckled at her remark. "What you talking about, Rosa?"

She had on a pair of tight fitting Daisy-Duke jean shorts. A pair of cutoff pants she loved to walk around the house and clean up in.

Rose went to her back pocket and pulled out a long thick plastic object in a wrapper like a candy bar. It was a pregnancy test.

Von jarred his head slightly. "What is this?" he asked.

"It's a pregnancy test. We got *a baby* on the way, Vonnie." Rosa said ecstatically. "A baby. You hit the jackpot." Another kiss. "And I'm so proud." Another kiss.

"**Huh!**" he exclaimed and placed both hands atop of his head. Von had his mouth wide open and appeared to be in disbelief.

"You mean to tell me I've got *two* babies on the way at the same damn time?"

"I'm hoping its *twins* I'm having. So that'll be *three*," Rosa responded on cue.

The effect of the words held a lingering reality to them, the possibility of that being true was a sure thing.

Whether Von knew it or not, he was going through a phase in his development and reproductive maturity when his fertility rate and sperm could experience an increase tenfold. The males on his father's side-the Savages-had these baby making abilities embedded into their genes. *Damn, I need to be careful.* He had a lethally impregnating weapon for a dick between his legs.

"What!" he let out in a shocking yet pleasing way.

Rosa kissed him once more. He still had his hand atop of his head. Von then walked over to have a seat on the couch and sat back to come to terms with the situation he had.

"Rosa, tell me how in the hell am I gonna explain this to Chloe?"

She looked over at him and jarred her head. "How you gonna explain this to, Chloe!?" she retorted. "Vonnie, *you're* the man. *You're* the boss. *You* tell *us* what the fuck to do. We don't tell you. *That's* how you explain it to her. You just say it! Not to mention, she's the one who said she wanted an open relationship. So it shouldn't be too hard to make her aware of what you got going on."

Von's phone vibrated. He was familiar with the number showing on his caller ID.

This nigga called at the right time. I need to talk to him anyway. I'm sure he's got some advice to give me, Von conversed with himself.

It was his father calling on video, so Von answered.

"What's good, pop! How you been, OG?"

"I've been good, son. No complaints. What about you?"

"I'm glad you called. I'm at one of my young jawn's crib."

"Talking bout the one you had in the car with you coming from the game that night not too long ago?" the father asked, referring to Monyetta.

"Nah-Nah-Nah, pop. Not her. Another one," Von responded.

"I heard that Vonnie!" Rosa playfully chimed in.

Von was on speakerphone.

"Oh shit!" he let out with a chuckle and smile. He kept the phone on speaker as it was.

"I didn't get you in any trouble did I, son?"

"No more trouble than I'm already in, pop. And that's what I need your advice about, OG. I've got a mean situation to deal with. From a relationship standpoint. Not the legal thing," Von made his father aware.

"What you got a baby on the way?" Hound Jr. let out with a smile.

"How about two?"

"Twins? Boy, you got lucky, didn't you?" His smile continued.

"Nah. Two different females."

"Oh! That part. They know about each other or they don't?"

"They do. But here's the crazy part to it all."

"What's that?"

"They're cousins."

The father jarred his head at the crazy revelation.

"You got it goin' on, don't you? Just be sure you got your dollars up, son, to take care of your seeds. And keep your own spot to live. That way you don't have to worry about one if 'em getting mad at you and kicking you out... find you a spot in the suburbs somewhere maybe up in Bucks County. And don't let nobody know where you live. You hear me?" His father properly advised.

"I do, pop. And that sound like something I definitely can do."

Rosa was listening in on everything that the father and son exchanged in words. She'd felt some type of way about the game the father gave to Von because she knew the worked to get Von to move in the way she wanted him to would soon be complicated. And she didn't need that.

"You know mom is home, right?"

"Drip mentioned something to me. That's why I called you, to get her new number."

Von provided his father the contact information to reach his mother.

"And how your grandmom doing? Mrs. Edna?"

"Oh, Nana good, pop. I'm surprised you asked about her. Grams tell me all the time how much I favor you," Von responded with a smile at the thought of his grandmother.

"Me and your granny always been cool, son. She liked me. Still do. She always wanted me and Lilly to settle down and get married."

"So what happened?"

"I wasn't ready for all of that at the time, son. Your dad was too caught up in the streets you know. But look, text me your mom and grandmom's numbers. And where this young jawn at you laid back with?" His father asked about Rosa.

"Oh, you wanna see what type of taste I got, huh?"

"Yeah," Hound Jr. responded delightedly.

"What type of taste buds in females you got, son?" he further said.

"Aye Rosa! My pop wanna speak with you and me together," he called out for her.

Rosa made her way to the living room.

"Yes, sweetie?"

"Come have a seat with me for moment, please. Let's talk with my pop for the time being," Von told her, so she did.

The three engaged in the desired conversation, having a good time talking on the phone, going over a lot of topics before ending the call.

Von and Rosa then began to talk over a few things.

"What's the other issue you wanted to speak with me about, Rosa? Since we got that part out the way," Von stated.

"Oh yeah. The thing I wanted to relate to you. My cousin, Tito, had a lot of questions about you. For some reason, he believes you knew about it or had something to do with my brother being killed. But, I told him there's no truth to that," Rosa stated.

136

"What! Why the fuck would he think that? And if that's the case, why he didn't say something to me about it when I showed up to pay my respects at your brother's funeral?" Von vented. He was now angered about Tito uttering his name.

"I don't know. And I didn't want to, but I had to let him know *you* and *me* were together in New York at the time when my brother was kidnapped and killed. So there was no way you knew anything about it or had anything to do with it."

"I know that's fuckin right! And I'm tired of Tito bringing up my name like that!"

"Don't worry about it, Vonnie. He wanted to know more, so I had him call the hotel where we stayed to check for himself. Both our names were on the reservation, remember?" Rosa reminded.

"I still need to speak with him one-on-one about it. He's done this one too many times now, Rosa. And we need to talk. What's his new number?" Von demanded.

"Vonnie, that's over with. You don't—"

"Rosa, what is Tito's number?" he cut her off to reiterate.

She gave him a stern look. "I'm gonna give it to you but not until you calm down. Not while you're pissed off like you are now. I don't want to create a problem between the both of you. That won't be good," Rosa stated.

"Look, I'm about to go for a moment, a'ight. I'll be back tomorrow."

"No, Von! I want you to stay here with me for a little while longer. Maybe all night. I just revealed to you that we got *a baby* on the way. That you're gonna be a daddy. Why you seem like that's not important to you?"

"I didn't say that."

"No. But your body language did."

"Stop speculating, Rosa. That ain't good and I told you, I'll be back. I got business to handle. A'ight," he stated emphatically.

"Promise me you'll be back? Tonight? Not tomorrow?"

"Rosa, look, I got business to handle. And you know I'm coming back. I'm obligated to. Now give me a kiss and let me go. Okay."

"Promise, Vonnie. I don't want to be here by myself. You already know I ain't got no friends other than at work. And besides that, I got you now. And hopefully, you'll properly explain to Chloe what we got going, then she and I can be pregnant together with our first babies, get back to being solid, and have you to ourselves like we want to. How do that sound?" Rosa let out, wrapped her arms around Von for a hug before leaning in for a kiss.

"Like a good idea for me to continue and let you explain exactly how we need to do things moving forward," he responded then kissed her. "And I'll be back when I get back. I told you, I've got business to handle... money to make... and babies to prepare for. Just call me if you need me, Rosa. Okay," he lastly let out, then walked out the door.

While walking down the steps and making his way to the car, he couldn't believe what his eye had laid upon. It was Chloe, seated behind the wheel on the car. She'd caught Von then and there, leaving the apartment of her cousin. They locked eyes, and Von paused in his track. What the fuck had he gotten himself caught up in? He had no choice but to explain what he had gone on now, whether he wanted to or not. What story would he tell? Or would it simply be the truth?"

Chapter 20

Detective Bill Hilliard made it a priority to secure an arrest warrant for the person of one, Shayla Allen, to question about the shooting of Stephon Richardson and the shooting death of guy's daughter, Dedra Richardson.

Upon request, the DMV provided police with an up to date photo of Shayla, and they knew what she looked like. They also had an address to her sister, Cori's house. A raid unit was formed to hit the location and apprehend Shayla. They moved in to get her.

BOOM!

The battering ram caved in the door at four a.m. The cops were heavily armed and fully equipped. All precautions were taken.

"Police! Police! We got an arrest warrant!"

"Everybody in the house, get down on the floor and keep your hands where we can see them!" the lead squad officer yelled out.

They stormed through the house from room to room, finding two people there, one in each of the two rooms. It was Cori and hers and Shayla's aunt, Shirley Allen.

"What the fuck going on?! Why y'all all up in my place like this! Who you looking for!" Cori yelled out to them in distress.

They were manhandling her while putting the cuffs around her wrists behind her back.

"Shut the fuck up! We ask all the questions! Not you!" One of the officers chastised her with words.

"You hurting me! What are you doing! Why you pressing your knee on my back, officer? I'm pregnant!" Cori stated. She needed them to lighten up a little.

Reluctantly, the cop who dealt with her eased back with this level of aggression.

Shirley was cuffed as well and the both of them were taken to the living room and were forced to have a seat on the floor while a search was conducted. The cops were looking for guns and any other contraband they could find.

Bill then walked inside the house once any potential threat from those who dwelled there was no longer prevalent. He had a legal envelope in one hand. They contained the warrant and other profile information he had on Shayla. Photos as well.

Bill pulled out the picture and took a look at it then at Cori.

"Similar but not who I'm looking for," he stated.

"Who are you looking for?" Cori asked.

"We're trying to locate Shayla Allen. Do you have any relations to her?"

"If me or her are not who you looking for, then why are we still in these damn handcuffs?" Cori retorted.

Bill gave her a leery look, then responded to her remark.

"I see you have a problem with authority, don't you, ma'am?"

"How would you feel about being woken out of your bed at an ungodly hour in the morning to your door being kicked in? Would you like that?"

"That's not a problem of mine, ma'am. But back to what I originally asked. Do you have any relation to Shayla Allen? Would this be her residence?"

"Sir, I don't have anything to say other than for you to turn me and my aunt there a loose, ASAP! Because you have no reason to hold us here," Cori barked back in a sarcastic way.

"We've got something here!" One of the officers in the back room doing a search announced.

He then made his way to the living room with roughly 150 grams of heroin, each packaged in one ounce Ziplock bundles.

"Well, what do you know? You spoke too fast, didn't you? Don't look like you'll be going anywhere now, does it? But I'm homicide. Not narcotics. And that there looks like you're gonna have to be taken in and booked on possession with intent," said Bill.

Cori had nothing more to say. She and her aunt were then escorted to the police car and taken to jail.

The cops made it their business to trash the house before ending the search and leaving. They'd taken the cell phones Cori and Shirley owned and any other material of value that was perceived to be paid for by drug money.

In addition to Von being one from the crew who found themselves in trouble with the law, Cori and her sister now were too. Not to mention the fact that Cori stated she was pregnant. Von was the only person she'd been with. And he already had two babies on the way. He had more problems to deal with than he ever knew.

$$\$\$\$\$\$$

Later That Day....

Shayla received a call from her mother to let her know that Cori and their aunt had been arrested. She was also made aware that the cops had a warrant for her regarding a murder and that was the reason why they raided the house to begin with.

Ah man, what the fuck?! Shayla cursed to herself.

That was the second time in her life that she had felt that bad. Of course the first was when she was cut.

Shayla called up Cold Heart to put him up on game regarding the current situation. She and Tangee were already in the car the two owned together, on their way across the bridge to New Jersey to check into the same motel they had before.

He answered. *"What's good, Shay?"*

"Cold! Me and Tangee on our way back to the motel in Jersey as we speak. We got problems, homie... the cops raided this morning and they hit my sister's spot. She and our aunt got knocked, bro," Shayla stated.

"What motel? The same one from before?" he asked.

"Yeah! That one."

"Okay. I'll be that way shortly."

"A'ight. I'll text the room number to you after we check in."

"Bet."

Cold Heart killed the call at that point. He and Monk were together on the way to Monk's apartment atop of the game room. They had other problems to deal with as well. Drip got word from his police lieutenant friend Pervis that a confidential informant eyewitness reported to the homicide detectives that he and his girlfriend saw Trevon "Vonnie" Savage shoot a guy in the head, killing him. The Lt. Pervis had learned that the guy's name was Tobias Flowers. Drip wanted Cold Heart, Monk, and the other homie who was with Von that day, Jeff Toliver, to be extra busy trying to track down the snitch and put him away forever.

Cold Heart and Monk talked in person on how to better deal with all the problems the team were being confronted with. The two then made their way to New Jersey to meet up with Shayla and Tangee.

Once they'd made it to the motel, they went inside to talk with the girls.

"Shay, run this down to us about the raid," Cold Heart stated.

She repeated all she'd been told.

"What about you?" Monk asked Tangee.

"They not looking for you either, are they?" he further questioned.

"Not that I know of," Tangee responded.

"I'm missing something in this though," Monk stated. "Why did they raid? Did the cops mention anything to your sister?"

Shayla was asked a very specific question. She exhaled, then spoke on the subject.

"Cold! For some reason, the shit came back up again."

"What shit?" he asked with a confused look on his face.

Shayla agitated her trigger finger. She took Tangee by surprise with that one because Shayla hadn't mentioned anything to her about killing Dedra. She had instructions to keep her fucking mouth closed. At all cost.

"This shit," she responded.

"How the fuck they find that out?"

"I don't know. I can't tell you. My sister told my mom to tell me that's why they came with a warrant. It was homicide. They found her supply when they searched the house. So she *should* get bail soon. Today. Tomorrow. Next week," Shayla related.

"Y'all got some money put away, right?" Monk asked.

"We do," replied Shayla.

"Hold on to it. Keep it put up for when you'll really need it. We'll put up the bail money for your sister. This gonna come outta Vonnie's pocket since part of the situation from this his and Cold's crew," Monk stated as he eyed Shayla and Tangee directly.

"Do Von even know about this yet?" Cold Heart asked.

"Nah. I called you first since I'm aware of the other issues he has on his plate to deal with. And I feel more attached to you. More than likely, Cori gonna let him know. I think them two acquainted in a special way anyway," Shayla informed.

Tangee looked over at her with a smile. She knew Cori had a serious crush on Vonnie.

"And not only that, my sister's pregnant. We definitely gotta get her out of there."

"Say what! You don't say," Tangee exclaimed with a pleasing smile.

Out of curiosity, Tangee asked Monk a pointed question. "I ain't never seen you around. Who you?"

Monk smiled at the pretty brown skinned cutie. "I'm Monk. Vonnie's people. Nice to meet you," he expressed, then extended his hand to shake Tangee's. She had a magical feel to her skin that appealed to Monk.

"I'm assuming since you're Vonnie's people, you're a Savage too, huh?" asked Tangee.

"For sho! I don't know how you knew."

"I see the similarities. You're a handsome guy, Monk. Just thought I'd let you know," Tangee complimented.

"You look nice yourself. Here...Lock my number in. Hopefully, the both of us can get acquainted with each other."

"That sounds like something I can get into."

"Well, if I'm able to get you into it, I'mma be sure to do all I can to not let you get out of it. You feel me on that?" declared Monk while maintaining strong eye contact with Tangee.

She grinned at the powerful level of charm Monk poured on. She then locked in his contact information in her phone.

Shayla and Cold Heart smiled at one another behind the apparent hook up between the two of them.

"Oh yeah, Cold, I almost forgot. My sister got Von's car parked in the storage. We gotta get her keys from the property down at the county jail and get bro car for him," Shayla said.

"We'll do that. And look, Tangee, if Cori don't get a bond by the weekend, I'm gonna need you to go and visit her, to get the full details of what we need to know. A'ight," Cold Heart stated.

She looked over at Monk and he nodded his head to approve.

Within that one instance, Tangee willingly put herself under the authority and management of Monk directly, while Shayla maintained that under Cold Heart. And at the moment Cori was bailed out, she would be under the dictation of Von.

It was strange how that work out but the three girls-Cori, Shayla, and Tangee-matched perfectly well with Von, Cold Heart, and Monk. And on the flipside of that, the other three girls-Ayonna, Monyetta, and Tiona-were already in their lives, and a lot of progress was being made by the guys with them.

The dude trio had themselves a girl on the high end of society and not in the streets and one on the low end side of society, who were all the way in the streets. Down for their nigga and with whatever they needed to be with for them. It couldn't be any better for a man to have a different female in a separate position, in the best way to help most. They had it going on.

$$$$$

Meanwhile...

Von had the duty to make the situation he had between Chloe and Rosa play out how he needed it to. On the day Chloe captured Von leaving Rosa's apartment, it was no better a time for them to put all the secrets they had on the table then and there. The time of playing the role of a grown man for Von was over. The time to *be* a grown man was at hand. Chloe imposed the issue on him.

She'd gotten out the car nonchalantly, closed the door, and stood and looked at Von and at how he would react to her appearing. She had her arms down by her side and a blank look covering her face.

Rosa looked out of her living room window and noticed her cousin.

"OH shit! Chloe! What the fuck?!" She uttered in a tense whisper to herself.

Rosa then walked to the door, opened, and stepped out onto platform to observe what was about to go on, if anything at all.

"Vonnie. Please tell me what's really going on? And you can keep it real with me about it. I'm not mad. Okay?" Chloe stated.

Von slowly shrugged his shoulders and produced a puppy dog look on his face. "What you wanna know, Chloe? I'll tell you everything."

"How about we go inside, and we all can have a conversation?" Chloe suggested.

The both of them began stepping towards the direction of Rosa's apartment door. She stood ramrod and jarred her head at the two while looking on, confused of what they had going on. Once coming to an understanding of what was occurring, she politely walked back into the unit and took a seat on the couch to wait for Von and Chloe to enter. They did so.

No one spoke a word and the silence of the room created space to think. Mostly of what would be said by each of them and how they would respond.

Chloe broke the mood with her voice. "Well hello to you, Rosa."

"Hey, Chloe. How are you?"

"I'm fine. What about you?"

"I'm good. I'll be doing better once we address the elephant in room," Rosa stated, getting straight to it.

"That would be a good idea. Vonnie, you wanna clarify a few things for me and my cousin? You can begin by explaining to me why you are here and without me knowing about it," Chloe said.

Chloe and Rosa both looked over at Von for his response. He remained standing while Chloe had taken a seat across from Rosa.

"This would be a good time to say what you need to say now, Von. Exactly how we talked about it," Rosa expressed to him.

"Wait a minute. What! That sounded like you two were already comfortable with one another. Are you?" Chloe said, doing her best to maintain her cool.

"And why are you here?" Chloe then added.

"A'ight look. I don't know how to lie or play any games with anyone of you. And we gonna keep this shit real and straight to the point," Von said.

"Me and Von been fucking, Chloe. All right. And he been staying over with me a few nights when he had the time to."

Rosa didn't hesitate to let it out. Now it was on Von to explain.

Chloe and Rosa turned their attention to him and anticipated his reply.

"How true is this, Trevon?" Chloe asked.

"Ok, look, it's true. But I didn't stop caring for you while me and Rosa played. And by the way you was the one who wanted an open relationship, Chloe. And you didn't clarify who was off limits. Now did you?"

Chloe paused extensively to think over all she may had said at the time she made the decision to express to him her desire.

"NO. I didn't. But Von, you *should've* known better than to go for my own damn cousin. Why would you do that?"

Von shrugged his shoulders and pursed his lips. "Because… I *could* and I wanted to be entertained by someone who was also like you. I know you remember all those times I told you I wish you had a twin who could be a *sister-wife,* don't you? Who's better than Rosa for that?"

He had a bit of humor to his explanation, causing Chloe and Rosa to chuckle and giggle at his remark.

"Chloe… Look. We're gonna keep this as peaceful, as respectful, and as cordial as possible. Okay. We can't get mad about any of this. And we've gotta let Vonnie dictate to us, how he wants things to be. Not us to him. Can we agree on that?"

Rosa and Von look over at Chloe for response.

"Hold up for a moment, Rosa. Let me make this clear. If I may. Vonnie is *my* dude. Okay, you only *borrowed* him for a fuck or two. And I get that. It was me who opened the door for him to explore his options. But let's not forget he's **mine**. And I don't get mad, petty, or even. I get *ahead*. For the record," Chloe set the record straight emphatically and in a calm tone.

She'd rendered Rosa at a loss for words.

Von spoke up. "Since you asked me why, I need to ask you, why are *you* here?"

"I'll let Rosa answer that for the both of us," Chloe stated.

Von turned to look at Rosa.

"Rosa. It's on you," he stated.

"I called her and asked her to come over, Von. I was so ready for us to do as we are now," Rosa explained. "But I didn't expected you to still be here when she arrived."

Von jarred his head at her reply. "Are you serious?"

"I am."

"Why would you do that?" Von demanded to know.

"It's because, Vonnie... I had to be the one to clear your name. I know for a fact you didn't have anything to do with my brother dying. How could you? We were together in New York at the time. And our cousin, Tito, wouldn't let up off it until he knew the whole truth. While you was up in Williamsport, he had me and Chloe together talking over everything. And you know we wouldn't lie to Tito, Vonnie," Rosa said.

"And not only that, I found *this* in your pants pocket," Chloe stated, then produced a meal receipt from the restaurant inside the hotel where Von and Rosa stayed.

"I called the hotel to know whose name was on the reservation list. I pretended to be Rosa. Me and Tito called together. And not only that, you told me out your own mouth you brought in the New Year with somebody else. In *New York*," Chloe revealed.

"And when Tito asked me a few question related to you, I told him about the trip to New York. I only confirmed what he already knew," Rosa made him aware.

"And I was there with Tito while the conversation between him and Rosa went on," Chloe chimed in to say. "The both of us. Me and Rosa together."

Von continued to stand and had a dumbfounded look on his face before getting vocal once more.

"Okay so, since we got all that out the way, what about the more serious stuff we need to clear the air on?" Von asked, looking back and forth at Chloe and Rosa, one to the other.

"What more *serious* stuff? You mean the part about me being pregnant? Or the part about me knowing your business is the underworld?" Chloe let out first.

"Rosa, I'm pregnant with Von's baby. And I know he deal drugs. And making a lot of money now. There, I let her know. Now your turn, Rosa," Chloe said confidently.

"Chloe... I—ah... I'm pregnant with Von's baby too. This was the serious thing I told you I wanted to tell you in person. Not over the phone. And you swore on grandpapa and promised me that you wouldn't get pissed. And I know about Von's business in the hustle game too. I've been to the spot in upstate as we've spent time together," Rosa made her cousin aware.

Chloe lowered her head and shook it from left to right in disgust. As bad as she didn't want to, she had no choice but to respect Rosa for letting her know. She couldn't get mad, and she couldn't make it her business to pick a fight. Neither of the two didn't want to risk losing their pregnancy behind emotions but instead put the pressure on Von to man up and eat the responsibility by paying for his pleasure.

Both the girls took side looks at Von and waited for him to say something.

"So what you gotta say for yourself, Vonnie? You got what you wanted. Now the question is, what you intend to do with the wish you've been granted ?" stated Chloe.

"Yeah, Vonnie. You're the boss. Let's not forget. And you tell us what the fuck to do. Not the other way around so keep that in mind. And we hope you understand how bad we want these babies. You've got good genes and strong bloodline. You and your father are awesome. That Savage shit is what we want to keep in our lives," Rosa expressed with a bright vibrant smile.

"Shit! What more do I need to say! Y'all already done put me on the spot and everything on front street. So...it is what it is. I'm happy with how we dealing with this. The both of you good with how we dealing with this. We all good with how this turned out. Blood is thicker than water , so why *not* keep me in the family to y'all-selves, you know. Now I gotta get this motherfuckin' money up and put it in a safe place to make sure my babies are gonna be taken care of," stated Von.

"Damn right, you do. And keep in mind what your pop said to you about keeping us in our own place, and you one of your own. Because we deserve that. And we're gonna go through some serious mood swings throughout this pregnancy. And we don't need to be taking out our frustrations on you," related Rosa. "And come on... sit down. Have a seat. And let's continue to make merry about it all," Rosa declared as she stood. Von strolled to the couch where they sat, with the cousins welcoming him in the space between the two of them. They continued to talk and make plans for the future.

Chapter 21

Eight Days Later...

Cori made a court appearance for bail and was granted a $250,000 bond. Monk and Cold Heart notified Von and he made it his business to put up the money to have his other pregnant girlfriend bonded out. Tangee was the one to pick her up at the front entrance of the jail and immediately took her to hers and Shayla's mother's home to see her two kids and to be sure the money she had her mother keeping for her was still in its amount and place. Cori had $50K tucked away. That was money she'd made from doing hair, nails, and selling heroin. Her ambition was to save enough money to lease a building and convert it to a hair and nail salon. Although suffering an arrest, her plan was still in place. Cori and Von reconnected for the first time since her arrest. They were in Von's Dodge Magnum--the black one and not the rental—and were on the highway headed to Williamsport to lay low at the apartment they shared. Apparently, the police did nothing on the case regarding the shootout that claimed the life of the guy Pac-Man and the other. They'd merely chalked it up a as gun battle between two drug gangs with two being killed. There was no identity on anyone involved, and no calls by eye witnesses to report information. They had nothing and left it alone. Completely.

The Philly dudes who were on Von's side made their way back to Williamsport as well. They'd gotten smart in a lot of ways by forming friends with cats who were from

Williamsport, supplying them, and they all began to get money together. Everybody was happy when everybody ate. Von's homie, Ron, made the right decision in that regard and a lot of the tension and resentment towards their crew by the street niggas born and raised there, had died down by business being increase. That was the best thing to do in order to not have so many people going up against them.

Von and Cori had a much needed conversation during the ride. He also was putting to the test the newly constructed compartment that had been hallowed out in his car. Monk contracted the job to build the stash box for Von at the time the headlight was fixed. The space had six kilos of H tucked away inside. This amount was to be enough to hold them down for the time being until Drip's Mexican connection— Alex Hernandez and elder brother Emilio—returned from their country with product. The cartel they were a part of suffered a hit down below the border and the trafficking route was on fire from American authorities.

Cori was situated comfortable in the passenger seat and feeling good at the moment. She had the music at a low volume with her favorite album playing on repeat. It was the *Scorpion* album by Eve. The track *Be Me* took her mind and feeling to a good space. She was the one to initiate the talk they needed to have.

"If only you know how much I missed you, Von. I had you and my kids on my mind the entire time I had to go through that situation," she expressed.

"I missed you too, Cori. I really did. And I know you may have thought I was gonna let you hang out to dry. But I couldn't do you like that. You been around since day one of this hustling sit. And it ain't no doubt in my mind if or not you down with me and down for me. Like I told you before, I *know* you are. We just need to keep it moving the way we are, stacking this money and coming up with a plan to start a legit business together. I know this dope dealing shit not gonna last but so long. And we don't need all these legal situations piling up on us. You feel me?" Von responded.

The honesty he held within him came out in a way with his elaborate reply.

"And you know I do, Vonnie," Cori replied, stroking him tenderly along the cheekbone with the tips of her fingers.

She continued. "But I need to know how much you're down for *me?* How *serious* are you about what we have? You willing to speak on that?"

"Why not. This is a good time to go over a few details on a deeper level. What exactly do you wanna know?"

"What exactly do I wanna know? Hmm, let me see. How about this? You ever had thoughts about being a daddy? Do you want kids?" Cori asked in an easy tone of voice.

Von turned his head slowly to have a look at her. He then placed his focus back on the road. With Von never being the one to blatantly lie to anyone when there was no need to, he felt the necessity to let Cori know what was going on in his life with Chloe and Rosa. He was hopeful Cori wouldn't flip the fuck out on him there in the car. Especially not with him having those kilos of heroin in his possession and on the run from police behind two murder charges they wanted him for.

"You want me to be straight up with you?" Von asked.

"Like a motherfucka, baby… I do. No pun intended with those last two words."

Von sighed and exhaled then proceeded to speak his truth.

"Look Cori, you know I'm gonna keep shit all the way gutta and real with you, right."

"I don't want it no other way, Von. I'm a big girl. I can take it however you give it to me," Cori stated emphatically.

"I've got two babies on the way now by two different girls," he revealed.

She jarred had at his words and gave him a stern look. Cori then lowered her head and shook it from side to side. She raised her head once more to have a look at him, then offered a response.

"You know what? Fuck it. I did say I'm a big girl, and I can handle what you have to tell me."

"Yes you did."

"And I don't have no choice but to accept your truth. I'm the one here with you now. We got a place together. And we getting to the money like we suppose to. Von. So guess what? I'm ok with it. Just don't get brand new on me. And be sure that you treat me *and* our baby with the same level of love and respect as you do those other two girls if not more," Cori stated.

Von jerked his head at the key words she had in her reply.

"*Our baby?* What you mean by that?"

"I mean it just how it sound. *Our* baby, Vonnie. We gotta baby on the way too. I'm pregnant, Von. I wanted to wait until the right time to tell you. Now has become that time."

"Say what! You bullshittin', right?!" Von asked ecstatically.

"I'm pregnant... the last time we had sex, I got pregnant. And I'm hoping my baby will come first. That way I can say that I gave you your first child. How does that sound?" Cori asked with a smile and a lot of positive energy.

"Oh shit! My black ass definitely gotta stepped my game up now. All these babies on the way and only a few months to get my act together. Thank you for being honest and real with me, Cori. We're gonna be aight. Okay. I promise," Von let her know. He then leaned over to give her a kiss.

Cori crossed her arms and layed back in the seat, producing a loving smile. She felt good about letting him know and about the direction that their relationship was going. She only hoped from that point to have a positive outcome in the court from her case she'd caught, and that they'd hustle and make enough money sooner rather than later to go legit. And she hoped for the healthy birth and arrival of their baby. Maybe, just a maybe, all she'd wished for would be granted in due time.

$$$$$

The economy of the country was on the rebound slowly but surely. The Obama administration issued numerous bailout grants to major brand name corporations, and many other foundation industries that were severely destroyed by the recession. Opportunities for real estate investors and property developers were everywhere, and Drip was looking to cash in any way he could. He was busy buying up foreclosed houses and commercial buildings in the North Philly area like he had once before. He also had an itch and desire to open a club and a sports bar somewhere in the hood where the area was being built up and transformed in a good way. Drip may had been a dude who was long removed from the streets, but he still had his heart and vision planted heavily in the streets. He wanted to explore the possibility and set out to do so.

Drip, Body, and their other homie, Animal, were together in Drip's Range Rover. He was the one doing the driving for the day in his own vehicle, and they were out and about cruising around North Philly, looking for a building he buy then could convert to a club or either a sports bar. He really wanted the bar first, to gain the knowledge and experience, and then do the club thing.

The three discussed the possibilities, beginning with Drip.

"What y'all think about us getting a building to turn into a sports bar?" he asked.

"Those things there are always gonna do good, I think," Animal responded first.

"Damn sure do. Look how long the Eagles Bar been up and going. That'll be something good to get into. But where?" Body chimed in.

"That's why we out and looking now. I always wanted to get into the bar business. We can make that happened now. Finally," stated Drip.

"No doubt, homie. What name did you came up with?" Animal asked.

"I was thinking maybe, Ozone Sports Bar and Grill. What you two niggas think about that?"

"That's a catchy name. It sounds attractive," Body stated first.

"That does sound like fire. And I know how you like to do it and add your own personal touch to things. But where?" Animal asked.

"We on the way to the spot now. I saw in the classified section of the *Philly Inquirer* that the building's on Sixth and Spring Garden, what used to be Palmer's Social Lounge, was now up for sell," Drip made them aware.

"That's a decent location there too, Drip. Not too far from Delaware Ave, where all the clubs are lined up on. The Ozone could get some of the business traffic from there," Body said.

"Exactly! That's the idea I had in mind anyway," proclaimed Drip.

Not too much longer, they were at the site of the building. They got out and walked up to the front door of the structure. There was three levels to it.

"I've spent many Thursday, Friday, and Saturday nights up in this spot here. Had a good time every visit. I know what the inside looks like. It used to have pool tables and a bar on the third floor. A large dance floor on the second level. And a main bar with standing space on the bottom floor," Drip stated while pointing a finger though the glass window of the entrance door.

Drip then looked into his phone for the contact information of the agency who carry the responsibility of selling the building. It was still early in the day, around four p.m. on a Wednesday.

"Hopefully, I can go hard and buy this building, renovate it to be what I want it to be with the grills and stoves and fryers and have it opened by the start of the football season in September," Drip said, making his intentions very clear and to the point.

"Shit, ain't nothing to it but to do it, bro. Let's get it going," commented Body.

"And then you can use this location as an office like you want to, you know. Do lunch and handle business and complete deals. What better way to do that than in your own place? Once you're able to shape it and remodel it how you see fit," Animal egged him on.

Drip took a look at both of his associate homies, smiled convincingly, and nodded his head passionately to indicate *yes.*

They all got back into the S.U.V. Body was behind the wheel now while Drip took the passenger seat and began to make calls concerning his interest in the building, and Animal situate himself in the rear. They were on their way to meet up with Monk; he had money to turn over to Drip. The young brother was with his girlfriend, Ayonna. They were at the Eagles Bar having wings and a few drinks. Drip had him spying on the place, so to help him get a better idea on how a sports bar was to operate. A smart move for a smart dude.

The Eagles Bar was located on the corner of Germantown and Erie Aves. This particular spot was by far the most popular bar and hangout destination of all the black neighborhoods sport bars. And yes, black owned and operated.

Drip and his two homies arrived. They exited the Range Rover and entered. Body and Animal took seats close to the door while Drip walked over to be with his brother and his girlfriend.

"What up, bro? How are you?" Monk greeted as he stood to his feet. The two dapped one another and then hugged tightly.

"How are you bro? I'm good on my end. Hey, Ayonna," responded Drip.

"Hey, bro-law. Nice to see you again," the hot cutie of Monk's returned the greeting.

"Nice to see you again as well. Monk been taking care of you properly, hasn't he?"

"Absolutely. He keeps a smile on my face," she said, then raise her hand to show off the new diamond friendship ring Monk gifted her with. She now had three of them. Ayonna had a necklace to match as well.

"I see. You gotta be sure to continue to do your part too. Love is a two way street. Don't ever forget that. Two can go along way by keeping to that understanding," Drip expressed as he took his seat with them.

"Y'all excuse me. I'm gonna go to the bathroom," Ayonna said, then excused herself to allow the two brothers to discuss business.

"So what the move is on your end, Monk?"

"I've got four hunnid K in my car out there for you now."

"That's what's up. How is the crew doing? Everybody good? And you already know I got Vonnie up in Williamsport building up the business one that end," said Drip.

"Everything good on my end, but not so good on the other," Monk stated.

"Not so good!" retorted Drip, causing his head to jolt.

"Nope. One of the girl's on Vonnie's team. On the run. And one, not too many days ago, got knocked with some product. She had to post bail. They so happen to be sisters."

"What the fuck *they* got going on?"

"From what I know, the cops raided the house looking for the one who got a body charge–"

"A body! Nah-Nah-Nah! They doing *way* too much now. But go ahead and finish explaining," Drip urged Monk.

"But yes, the raid. They was looking for one and found some work the house. That's how the other one got booked. The cops only want to question her. The dude who supposed to be the main witness, ain't around no more. He gone forever, Body and Animal can tell you more about that, if they haven't already."

"Yeah, they told me something about Cold having to snatch up some nigga and getting rid of him. Is that the body they want to question her about?"

"Nah not that one. Dude was one of the people who got shot. But it was his daughter who died. If you remember back 'round Christmas time, they had it on the news about a little girl being shot and killed."

"Yeah, I do. That's what they want to question her about?"

Monk shook his head to indicate *yes*.

"Did she do it?" Drip asked.

Monk indicated *yes* by the nod of his head once more.

"You had the chance to talk to her about everything?" asked Drip.

"Yeah, I did. Her and the chick she be with are over in Jersey at the motel keeping low that way."

"That's a good thing. Now we gotta figure out what to do from here. What do you think need to go on?"

Monk brainstormed for a moment to think over every possible scenario to bring an end to the drama Shayla had to face. He knew it wouldn't be a good thing to provide his opinion so fast to Drip, until he himself had all the facts. Also, Monk knew Cold Heart and Shayla had something going on with one another. And he was beginning something new with the best friend and sister-like figure of the girl as well. So therefore, he didn't want to cause a wedge between their relationship. Monk bought time for Shayla.

"Give me the chance to talk to her again so I can know the whole story. I'll get back to you then, bro. The girl is a diehard team player, Drip. I know this for a fact. And she been down with Vonnie and them since way back. I know shorty and Cold kinda close with one another too," explained Monk.

"A'ight. You be sure to do that, bro. But keep this in mind though. If shorty turns out to be more problems than she's worth, we can't keep her around. Especially not with no goddamn body charge they looking for her on!" Drip stated as he stood to his feet to leave.

Ayonna was now in their presence once again.

"Wait here for a moment, babe. I'll be back in minute, okay," Monk said to her.

"Okay, sweetie."

The four men made their way to the parking lot. Monk opened the trunk to his Benz to retrieve the cash he had for Drip. He had the money bundled and stuffed in an all-black *Prada* tote bag.

Monk grabbed hold of the handles on the bag then passed it to Drip.

"Here you go, bro."

Drip accepted, then handed over to Body. He and Animal took a seat in the Rover until the two brothers were done talking.

"Oh yeah. I gotta let you in on something. Before long, we gonna have our own sports bar to give this one here a run for its money," Drip affirmed confidently.

"Word!" Monk responded. "So, that's why you had my spying."

"Word! We're gonna call it, The Ozone. It's gonna be a bar and grill."

"That's what's up there, bro. I can't wait to experience what that jawn has to offer. For real," Monk expressed.

"No doubt, me either. But look, you be easy on your end, bro, and hit me up if you need me, aight."

"For sho', bro."

The two then dapped and embraced once more. Drip got in his ride and they drove off while Monk made his way back inside the bar. Everyone continued on about their day as planned.

Chapter 22

The friend and now worker of Von's, Jeffery Toliver aka "JT", managed to make a lot of progress near the corner of 8th and Diamond. This was the location where Von had popped the guy Kavon Lassiter in the head for banging into his car.

JT brought along three of his cousins to set up shop there with him. For some reason, the guy, Tobias Flowers, hadn't been back around too much. Most likely, he handled his business over the phone and wanted to avoid any confrontation with Von and crew at all cost. He didn't know if or not word had gotten out there that he and his girlfriend ratted to the police about what they witnessed on the day of the shooting and he didn't feel the need to find out the hard way. Tobias knew the Savage boys had connections and may have had cops on payroll. So he simply went about things in a different way.

JT was up to working two kilos now. He had it set up to where his cousins sold all the baggies and bundles while he sold weight at an ounce or more at a time.

JT had a customer he'd been dealing with for just over a month now. The guy bought an ounce the first time they'd done a deal; two ounces for the second and third times. And on the fourth deal, the guy ordered six ounces. That became the point in which his true identity and agenda was revealed. Turned out, dude was a federal agent and not the typical block dope hustler he posed as being. JT provided the guy the location to the house he stayed over near 7th and Montgomery. It was Thursday around nine a.m. and they went to get him.

Once they'd arrested JT upon a raid of the house, he was taken into the Federal Detention Center downtown and was interrogated. Two AR-15 rifles and four handguns were found in the raid as well, along with a half kilo of heroin. The federal agents discovered a cache of *Black Rhino* bullets in addition to the weapons and narcotics. They had more than enough to bury JT in Federal prison for no less than 30 years unless... he was willing to give up the people he worked for, and the person who'd supplied him with those firearms and 500 rounds of cop killer bullets. JT was more than ready to talk. Wear a wire. Take the stand. Whatever! He just wanted to do away with going to prison for all those years and not being there for his three year old daughter. He had a murder he wanted to make them aware of too. One that a personal friend committed.

"Mister Jeffery Toliver, I'm AUSA Fredrick Cox. I'll be the one most likely going to prosecute this case. You got yourself in some deep shit here, dude. Deep shit! You want to help yourself the best way you can??" stated the medium height, medium build, clean shaven African-American military veteran with a low crew cut that was accompanied with splashes of gray.

"I really don't have a choice, if I intend to be free to see my daughter grow up," JT responded.

"So you're a father, huh? How old is your daughter?"

"She's three."

"Three. *Mmm-mmm-mmmm.* Such a shame," retorted Cox, shaking his head from side to side to express disgust.

"If you don't tell us what we wanna know, that little three year old you got will more than likely be *one hundred and three* by the time you make it home. So I highly suggest you get busy telling us what we want to know or you can kiss your life goodbye. You've got an option. Which side you choose?"

JT was given an ultimatum. He accepted the offer made by the government.

$$$$$

One Day Later...

The lead homicide detective over the North Philly district, Bill Hilliard, got a call from the U.S Attorney's office. They had a guy in custody who had firsthand knowledge related to a murder case he was over. JT was alongside the shooter. The killer was his friend. And his name was Trevon Savage. Toliver wanted to help them solve the case, in exchange for a lighter sentence.

Bill and Valco made their way to the Federal building to meet with AUSA Cox and interview the witness they had in custody.

The three of them had JT surrounded in the interrogation room and drilled him with a series of questions. Valco had his note pad on hand and was ready to cross reference with all JT had to say.

"Mister Jeffery Toliver, I'm Detective Bill Hilliard and this is my partner, Valente Canelo. We are in the hopes that you don't have us here to waste our time or to stall the prosecution of you with the charges you have."

"Sir, I don't intend to waste your time in the least. I totally understand the mess I've got myself into. And I needed a way out."

"Let's just get straight to the point of why we're here. Shall we?" stated Bill.

"Let's do that," JT responded.

"What exactly did you see, and what exactly do you know?" Bill stated emphatically,

JT explained to them everything that took place that day. He provided names and distinctly described the incident.

"The guy I sold heroin for and the guy who pulled that trigger name is Trevon Savage," informed JT.

Both Bill and Valco jarred their heads at the mentioned of the name.

Valco went directly to his notes that had the name associated with it.

"What type of car does the Savage fella drives?" Valco asked.

"Dude got a sharp-ass black Dodge Magnum. That was the car the guy made a mistake and banged into. He only made an error so many people make on a daily basis," JT remarked as he lowered his head and shook it slowly.

"That's our guy, Bill. No doubt about it," said Valco.

Bill squinted his eyes, placed his hands in his pockets, and dug in with more questions. He, Valco, and AUSA Cox, were all standing around the table where JT sat.

"Give a description of what this guy Savage look like?" Bill uttered.

"He a young cat. Kinda tall. Dark in complexion in a way. Keep a low all around cut. A serious looking young guy. He'll make you think he's older than he is. But he's only seventeen soon to be eighteen."

"This definitely the guy we are looking for. He's been dodging us for a little while now. We just never knew what he looked like," said Valco.

"And how long you and Savage been knowing one another?" Bill asked.

"We been cool since childhood. Went to school together and all… me, him, and our other homie, Eunice."

"Y'all went to school together?" Bill retorted.

"Yes sir."

"High school?"

"That too. Simon Gratz High."

CLICK!

Valco snapped his fingers. He'd thought of an angle they could pursue to get the identity of the double murder suspect they wanted.

"I've got it, Bill. I've finally thought of how we can know what this Trevon Savage looks like."

"And how is that?"

"The school yearbook. We can go over to the high school he attended and get a copy of it. I'm sure he has to have a photo somewhere on his school records, right? Either a school ID or a photo in the year book," Valco declared.

"Exactly!" Bill stated enthusiastically. "How come we didn't think of that before, Valley? We're on it now, but back to you, Mister Toliver. You got a phone number to your friend Savage? We need to track his calls."

"He's my supplier. And my *former* friend. Of course I've got a contact to him… it's in my phone. I'm sure they took it in the raid of my place," JT responded.

"Can you get your hands on that for us please?" Bill asked of AUSA Cox.

"I sure can. We'll have Mister Toliver here provide the passcode to make our access easier. Then, get that information to you, ASAP," Cox responded.

"Sounds fine to us. But a couple more questions for you, Mister Toliver. Then we're done. At least for the day," Bill said.

"I ain't got no problem at all answering any question y'all need me to speak out on. I'm not trying to go to prison for the rest of my life behind a few guns and drugs. Especially not so when I know a thing or two about a murder and I know y'all take homicide way more serious than anything. Now that, I know," stated JT.

All three law enforcement officials looked at one another and smiled. JT held his head high and rotated it from one side to another in observance at their reaction from his comments.

"You're a smart man, Mister Toliver," Bill uttered. "We want to know do you know the name of Trevon's mother?"

"Everybody calls her Lilly. That's all I know."

They continued to question JT a little longer. Through the process, he was offered the opportunity to sign a "Proffer" agreement to fully cooperate with both state and federal authorities. The feds wanted JT to wear a wire upon him letting him free from lock-up for a time being. Then, once the amount of information they look to gain on the wire-tap from their new devoted confidential informant was up, JT would then go through the transition of being placed in the Witness Protection Program. The process could take months or maybe a year. The feds cared nothing about the safety and physical well-being of JT and his family. Their mission was to track down the supplier of the fentanyl laced heroin that JT was captured with; to find the source of the guns and lethal cop killer bullets he had; and to also assist Philly homicide on the murder(s) that the informant in custody had knowledge of. Their plan was in progress.

Chapter 23

One month Later...

Drip had Monk to take a trip to Williamsport to be sure their young troubled cousin, Von, had everything in order and properly functioning like expected of him to. Drip was all about handling his business, putting his finances in the right places, and eliminating problems. And being he'd helped Von, his father, and his mother in a major way, he wanted Von to work off his repayment and get his feet on solid ground once more, in the event he had to go away to do time.

Drip also wanted the female worker on their team, Shayla, to get out of the city and go upstate herself, to hustle and make money, preparing for the showdown with police when the time came. He didn't need problems in Philly from *wanted* people who sold product he supplied. Family, friend, or associates made no difference to him. Drip wanted them out the way. And he had Monk to ensure that they were.

Turned out, it worked to the advantage of Monk, Cold Heart, and Von. Because they had dealings with the three females who sold their drugs: Cori, Shayla, and Tangee.

Von and Cori were already in Williamsport. Cold Heart and Shayla made their way upstate next. With Monk and Tangee following suit later that week. The plan was for all six of them to spend two days together beginning that Thursday. But Monk wanted Tangee to himself to finally see what she was all about sexually and as a female companion.

His opportunity to have that moment was at hand. It was a Wednesday, and Tangee wanted it to be their official date night time from that moment moving forward. Monk had no problem with it.

Monk was a lot like his brother Drip in so many ways when it came to the females they'd chose to deal with. He immediately began to upgrade Tangee to fit the type of female he wanted her to be.

They went shopping at the *Cherry Hill Mall* following their dinner, making a few stops at high end clothing stores. Monk wanted Tangee to fully acquaint herself with *Fendi, Prada, Gucci,* and *Chanel.* Dude dropped $20,000 on her the very first shopping spree they'd had together.

Once Tangee's special treatment by Monk had ended for the day, the two took a tour of the city in his big body Mercedes Benz.

"This is a nice ride, Monk. It really is. And by the way, may I call you by your real name? I like it. A lot! *Shamar Savage.* That fits you. I feel like I'll have more of a special connection to you by using your actual name, instead of the one any random chick calls you by, if we're gonna do this. I ain't no random chick. On *no* level," Tangee stated.

"I'm ok with you calling me by my real name. If it's what you wanna do. And I wouldn't have shit to do with you if you were some 'random' female. I don't go for ordinary... I only fuck with *extraordinary.* I wouldn't give you any of my time, if I thought less of you," Monk responded.

"I like the way you put that. It really shows the type of person you are. You ain't no fake nigga, Shamar. You the type of dude who's all about your business... that shit must run in y'all's niggas bloodline or something... Von the same way. Is that's where he get it from? It runs in the family?"

Monk produced a smile at her words. He felt that too about her and wanted to seriously lay a foundation with Tangee. But before that was to go on, he needed to know more about shorty.

"How come I don't ever hear you talking about your family? Where's your mom and dad? You got any siblings?"

"Nah bruh. I ain't got no family other than my granny. My mom was a notorious junkie the majority of my life. She gave me up to my grandparents when I was born. And the nigga who supposed to be my *daddy*..." rage was now evident in her voice, "...he out there somewhere, I can't tell you. But granny Ruth is all I got. Other than Shayla and Cori. I've been staying with them on and off since seventh grade. Me and Shay been close since the sixth grade," Tangee revealed.

Monk took notice of the emotional turn the conversation was taking. He changed it up to lighten the mood.

"What about your past relationships? Your ex-boyfriends?" he asked.

"I ain't really had no boyfriends in my life. Only two that I messed with. I've only had sex maybe five times. My interest in a relationship didn't happen until the last year or so. I had to get through school to make my granny proud. I'm the only grandbaby her and my grandad had. He passed away when I was a twelve," Tangee explained.

"Understood. And you don't have to worry about me turning out to be a bullshit nigga in your life," remarked Monk.

"And you don't have to worry about me turning out be a bullshit *bitch* in your life, either, Shamar. Especially not with you spending on me the way you did. I never had a nigga to go into his money-bag on me the way you went into yours. I thank you and appreciate it."

"More where that came from, sweetheart... all you gotta do is keep true to who you are and keep true to me. That won't be too hard, will it?"

"Not at all, boo. Not at all."

They'd arrived at Monk's apartment studio atop of the gameroom. All the shopping bags they had were gathered and they entered the space.

Tangee took a look around Monk's domain in awe. His pad was laid. He had exclusive Italian furniture and decor all through the dwelling. Designer label material accompanied.

"Nice place as well. You've got good taste I see. I must be a very-very-very- lucky girl. You're a Godsend, I believe," Tangee expressed.

"I feel the same way about you, Tangee. You make me feel comfortable and special in your own way," Monk responded.

Tangee took a seat on the black colored leather couch, crossed her legs and arms, and leaned back into the chair, looking at Monk with a smile of admiration.

Monk turned on the TV for her.

"What you wanna watch?" he asked.

"I'm a huge fan of *Sex In The City*," she responded.

"What you got to drink on?" Tangee asked.

"Whatever you want to drink."

"I like white wine. Chardonnay. And I wouldn't mind taking a shower. I'm so ready to slide my ass and put my pussy into a pair of those *Prada* panties you brought for me. I'm ready to let you see this divine body I've been maintaining too. I've been preserving myself for a good nigga a long time now, Shamar," Tangee expressed in a confident manner.

"Well go on and pop your shit then, sweetie. I love it when I get that type of feedback, you know," Monk responded with a pleased smile and more energy.

"I've got new towels, new wash cloths, new everything. I want you make yourself at home, ok. I don't ever bring no one to my spot unless I'm really into them and really looking to have trust in them. I feel very good about you, Tangee."

Tangee stood to her feet and began getting out of the clothes she had on. She then folded them neatly and spoke again while doing so.

"I'm glad to know I've made that type of impression on you. And I put it on my life, Shamar, I'mma do everything necessary to keep this good impression at a high level. Ok," she let out while walking up to him.

Tangee kissed him slowly and passionately.

"You've got a *real* bitch in your life now." Another kiss. "Just so you know." One more kiss.

Tangee then made her way to the bathroom in her birthday suit. The plumped, round, and seductive ass of hers bounced enticingly up and down and from side to side, as she slowly sauntered down the short walkway from the living room.

Damn she's is a tight piece of work, Monk mused to himself.

He then went to his bedroom once Tangee was situated in the shower. Monk got undressed, only and kept on his boxer shorts and tank top shirt. After putting on a pair of slippers, he made his way back to the kitchen to make them a drink and prepared a bowl of fruit and a side dish of exquisite gourmet cheeses. Snack crackers were added to complement the cheese.

Shortly thereafter, Tangee exited the bathroom and found Monk situated in his room atop of the bed with their drinks and a snack. She had a towel loosely wrapped around her body. She'd used a portion of the men shower gel Monk had to lubricate. The brown sugar complexioned cutie smiled at him, then slow peeled back the covering to reveal her feminine ornaments. Tangee had shaved the day before, creating a landing strip design to her house of love. Her thighs were soccer fit, belly flat, and titties firm and bulging with thick hardened nipples. Tangee had Monk spell bound and enchanted with her awning aura and mesmerizing position of posture.

"You got one hell of a body," he complimented.

"Thank you. Now I wanna see yours," she responded.

Monk got naked while sitting on the bed. Tangee got atop and crawled slowly to the head area to meet Monk with a kiss. They both ate a serving of cheese and crackers, fruit, and drank half a glass of wine each.

"And now the part I'm pleased to get into," Tangee let out before going down on Monk to suck his dick. He was already semi-erect.

Monk stretched out the long way and allowed his manhood to stand at attention. Dude was working with a little something. The Savage family genetics for the males in their private area proved conquering. Monk was blessed with a nine inch piece of meat. Tangee grinned at the trophy that was now hers, going to work with pride and privilege.

Tangee passionately bobbed and pulled on his dick. She was determined to impress Monk, so that he'd make it his business to put her first before the other female or females she knew he had. At no time would Tangee go so far as to ask anything about another. Her grandmother Ruth had taught her long ago that men hated it when the female he's currently dealing with asked anything about another he's suspected or presumed to be dealing with. To men, that's a sign of weakness and a sign of jealousy. Characteristics a *confident* female should never have.

It didn't take long for Tangee to bring Monk to peak erection. She was now ready to fuck. Her pussy throbbed. The juices of her love pool had her wet as ever. While sucking Monk off, Tangee sensually caressed her own private, slowly running two fingers in and out to fully stimulate herself. She then straddled him. Her back straightened, protruding her breasts even more. Tangee had a silver belly piercing just above her navel. It sparkled from the dim light of the lamp.

At that point, she grabbed hold of those pretty breasts she'd been blessed with and pinched her nipples hard.

"You know how to turn a nigga on, don't you?" Monk expressed.

"You better know I do," Tangee responded while sitting the head of Monk's manhood at the entrance of her love box.

She then gently humped up and down a half inch at a time, working the large dick into her world. The love potion provided the right amount of lubrication, making access easy.

Tangee then palmed his chest muscles and planted her claw-like nails into him. Cori did a really good job on them as a nail technician. Her, Tangee, and Shayla often rotated their work to beautify one another.

"Ooh! You like to play rough a little bit too, I see. Just my way of doing things," Monk let out.

"I wouldn't have it no other way." The young tender couldn't contain all the pinned up sexual energy any longer. She began to get loose. It had been a long time since she'd had a dick stuffed in her and she had those intense ecstasy feelings return to her all over again.

Tangee rode the dick to the best of her ability, grinding in gyration, sliding up and down, rocking back and forth, until she'd reached her moment of clarity.

Suddenly, she shuddered as her orgasm took control of her body. Her eyes slightly rolled to the back of her head. She'd locked her talon like nails onto his pec muscles again and moved her pelvic in a rapid fashion to enhance the feeling she was experiencing. Monk's manhood was fully inside her. Deeply situated in Tangee's love tunnel. She exhaled a grand sigh of pleasure and provided a cheery smile at Monk.

"That felt sooooo good! I swear it did," she acknowledged.

"I'm sure it did. It's my turn now to know the feeling, sweetie," Monk responded, returning a smile of his own.

Tangee eased up from her straddle position, leaving a creamy thick frothy amount of her release all along the shaft of Monk's manhood. Her love foam was also clustered all around the front portion of her private. The sight of what she'd produced caused the both of them to smile more.

Tangee then lay on her back, spread her legs wide, and welcomed her Savage thug back into her world of pleasure. She was ready for the dick to penetrate her again.

Monk mounted, holding his large dick with his left hand, eager to put it back in, and stroked her hair with his right hand. He and Tangee maintained strong eye contact at the moment. A connection was made. One that would keep them together possibly for a long time to come.

At the point of fully inserting, Monk began to stroke slow. He had a motion of finesse to his love making skills, and then, his pace picked up. Monk had her legs pinned to the side of her head as he banged away. The tingling sensation felt so damn good to him.

Monk was now ready to blow his load. He pulled out of Tangee and came all over her belly and breasts. His cum was warm, thick, and gooey. Tangee massaged his release all over her body. Monk and Tangee laid flat on the bed. They tongue kissed. That happened to be an epic and memorable moment in the beginning stages of what they were seeking to establish. Monk had plans for them moving forward.

Epilogue

Two Month Later...

Von was at the apartment he'd put Chloe in. He and Rose went there together so they could talk and hold nothing back from one another. They were intent on putting it all out to her and no longer keeping secrets. The three of them wanted nothing to do with any activity or behavior that would make the situation toxic. And Von wanted those two to function and get along as well as they always had, so that they could have a healthy and positive pregnancy and could birth the babies they carried that he was the father of.

For the weeks, between the time they'd all came together to reveal what was going on, Chloe and Rosa made it their business to thoroughly look into the practice of polygamy. To their surprise, this particular lifestyle had many benefits to come alone with it. Something that they could definitely get into. And the two girls were again ready to place additional demands upon Von, so that he'd be able to fully understand the exclusive pleasure he now had to pay for. That was how they termed it. He had to "pay for his pleasure." And in paying for his pleasure he had no problem doing. God forbid anything was to take place to alter or prevent that.

Chloe and Rosa sat together on the love-seat in the den area, and Von took a seat on the large bean bag he had situated there. He liked the comfort the bean bag provided whenever he played the *Playstation* for hours at a time.

He opened with the line of conversation they were looking to have.

"A'ight, so look, I'm so happy to know that this is going a whole lot better than I initially thought it would, I gotta admit. I was scared as a motherfucker. Chloe, when you caught me at Rosa's house that day, I didn't know what the fuck to do. I thought you was about to get on my ass! I really did," Von said.

"Nah. You was good, Vonnie. You already had more than enough to deal with and I didn't need to complicate things. Besides, I know I wasn't gonna be able to stop you from seeing who you wanted to see and doing what you wanted to do. Now that you're in the world and on higher level than before. Your mom had a lot to do with me accepting and embracing the idea too. She explained how your dad was, and all she had to do to keep him interested," Chloe explained.

"Is that right? I'm glad to know that."

"When will I get the chance to meet your mom, Von?" Rosa chimed in.

"The both of us gonna do so soon," Chloe made him aware, as she turned her head to the right, locked eyes with her cousin, and smiled while explaining, "Or we can have her come here to meet with us while Vonnie's here too."

"That sounds better there," commented Von. "But look, I'm curious to know did you and Rosa ever talk about how me and her find a way to begin dealing with each other?"

Both girls took a look at one another. Being that Chloe was the one in Von's life first, she offered to expound upon the subject in as few words as possible.

"The thought never crossed my mind to ask about it, Vonnie, to be honest with you. It really don't matter. Besides, you had permission. And not only that, you did have enough respect to keep your interest in the family. And, me and my favorite female cousin got you to ourselves. So everything works out to your advantage. Why mess up a good thing?" Chloe said, while smiling from one to another.

Von and Rosa returned the same.

Rosa now piggybacked off what Chloe said. "She couldn't have put it any better Von. And now that we both have you, there is a lot of responsibility to go along with us."

"Geez! Tell me about it," he let out.

The girls giggled at his remark.

"You definitely gotta step your game up now, sweetie. Because we planning to move in together soon. Here in this apartment. And all that money you making with your hustling, we've gotta put some of it away to support the babies when they get here," Chloe stated.

"I understand, I really do. And we're gonna get busy doin' that next week. The money I bring in over the weekend gonna be the start-up to handle that. A'ight. But I've got this one naggin' issue on my mind I need to deal with as we move forward," Von stated.

"You talking about the thing with Tito, ain't you?" Chloe uttered, knowing exactly how Von thought and liked to approach things.

"You already know. Me and him need to have a one on one conversation. But he seems like he's too stubborn to talk with me. How he gonna put my name in some shit like that and not offer me the opportunity to straighten my name. I don't understand it. And everytime I had one of you get in touch with him to talk with me, he brushes you off," he shook his head. "We not gonna be able to move forward happily until this issue is gone. I'm so ready to deal with this shit. I really am."

"You know what?" Rosa got their attention. "How about we all just pull up on Tito's together and let him know now what we got going on. That way, we all can dead that then and there," she suggested.

"No doubt. Why don't we do that? Tito wouldn't have no choice but to let it go then once we pull up at the shop and reveal our reality," said Chloe.

"NO! We don't go to the shop. He'll have too many other people around him, and we don't need nobody other than us present, to hear what we have to air out. I want us to pull up on him at his house. The place where he's very comfortable and not on alert. He won't think it's a setup either. Because I'll be with you two and he no doubt trusts y'all," Von stated.

The two girls looked at one another in a serious way. They knew how much Tito was against anyone other than family coming to his house without his permission. But at the same time, if they were to ask him would it be ok to bring Von over to talk, he'd vehemently tell them *no*! So, Von's version would be the best route to take regarding the situation they were looking to do away with.

Chloe was more familiar with how Tito felt about the move they were about to make and offered to speak up if they proceeded with her suggestions.

"We can all go out to talk to him. If he has anything to say, which I'm sure he will, I'll be the one to speak up about it. Ok?" Chloe said to them.

"No doubt. Let's go," Von responded.

They all got to their feet and prepared to leave. The three of them exited the apartment and got into Chloe's car. Away they went.

$$$$$

Tito had a nice brick home just on the outskirts of Philly heading west. Chloe hopped on Interstate 676 from Interstate 95. Von had made a stop by his grandmother's home briefly, wanting to check on her. He hadn't done so in a couple weeks since his mother posted bail. From there they proceeded to Tito's.

The time was just past ten p.m. when they arrived. Tito's Navigator, the one he drove more than any of his other vehicles, was parked in the driveway. That meant he was home. So were his girlfriend and two daughters.

"Well we're here," Chloe said.

"Tito's gonna give us hell too, Chloe," Rosa uttered. "I can feel it in my bones."

"It don't even matter at this point. We gotta do what we gotta do and get this over with. For good."

Tito's nine year old daughter took a look out of her bedroom window and recognized Chloe's car. She'd seen the headlights when they pulled up. The little girl then opened the door to the living room as the three guests were exiting the car right at that time.

"Hey, Chloe… hey, Rosa!" Tito's daughter greeted them.

"Hey, Nivea! How are you?" Chloe responded.

Nivea then gave her two cousins a hug.

"Your dad here?" Rosa asked.

"Mm-hmm! He is."

"Come on. Let's go in. We need to see him," Chloe said.

They then stepped inside.

Nivea went to the backroom to notify her father that he had company. Tito made his way to the living room, holding his daughter as they walked.

Upon laying eyes on Chloe, Rosa, and *Von*, he was thrown into a state of shock. He thought he'd saw a fucking ghost! Tito instantly got heated.

"What the fuck?!" he yelled. His outburst startled little Nieva. "Go to your room baby. Okay." he ordered her.

Von did nothing but simply stood and stared at him. Von's intention was to only respond to all Tito had to say. Not initiate.

"Chloe! Rosa! Why the fuck y'all bringing this dude to my motherfuckin' home?" Tito hissed through clenched teeth.

Chloe offered to respond first. "Tito. We need for you to please calm down and hear us out. There is something very important we need to talk to you about. Ok"

"So why the fuck didn't either one of you call me about this?" he spat, pointing back and forth at both Chloe and Rosa.

"Because, Tito…We knew you wouldn't agree to this. And this is the best way to get your attention. A phone call wouldn't do. It had to be like this," Rosa chimed in.

Tito now looked directly at Von. "What's up, man?! What you got to talk about!" he directed to Von in a slightly aggressive way.

Chloe and Rosa both got quiet. They allowed Von the opportunity to speak.

"Tito, look. I came in peace. And I came to *speak* my peace. A'ight."

"Get on with it. I'm listening," Tito replied.

"A'ight, so look. I know my people took care of that debt for me I owed you. Problem solved. At least on that. And I know Rosa already told you me and her were together in New York City at the time somebody killed her brother. So ain't no way I could've done it. And I didn't have anything to do with it. There ain't no reason my name should be attached to that anymore," Von said.

"He's telling you the truth, Tito," Chloe cosigned.

"This what I'm tryna understand. Chloe, if dude's *your* boyfriend, why the hell would he be in New York… with *Rosa?* Your cousin?"

"It's because, Tito, to get straight to that point… Me and Rosa are both in a relationship with Von. To make a long story short."

Tito notoriously jarred his head. "What?!"

"I can't even begin to explain how this came to be. Just know that it's now our reality," Chloe stated.

Tito looked at Rosa to hear her take. She nodded to confirm *yes.*

"And also, if you must know more, the both of us are pregnant with Von's babies. And we're in the process of moving into the same apartment together," Chloe provided additional truth.

"You... you got to be bullshittin' me, right? You gotta be," Tito responded.

"She's not bullshitting, Tito. It's the truth," Rosa said.

Tito glanced at Von. Dude offered a smile of absolute satisfaction while slowly shrugging his shoulders and flipping his hands, palms up.

"Do you now understand why this conversation had to happen, and the bullshit beef between me and you need to stop? Right now? This day?" Von declared.

Tito's girlfriend stood at a distance and looked at them. She'd heard everything that was said, offering a half smirk, half smile.

"Y'all motherfuckas crazy! For real, y'all are! I should've known something *deeper* was going on between you two..." he pointed from Rosa to Von, "...from the way you hugged and carried on at Alfredo's funeral. How you didn't see that, Chloe?" stated Tito.

"Tito, me, Rosa, and Vonnie are past that now. Alright. We all agreed that the best way to remedy this, is to simply be together in a three-way relationship. Von..." Chloe pointed at him, "already knows he has a responsibility to pay for his pleasure. And we moving forward in the way we are," said Chloe emphatically.

"I'm doing my part, Tito," Von let out. "And I plan to hold us down to the fullest, for the sake of my babies they're gonna have soon. So...Can me and you end any animosity that exist between us and keep it pushing peacefully? I hope that's not asking too much, is it?" Von uttered, then extended his hand to shake Tito's.

Reluctant at first, however, Tito went on to shake Von's hand. In the eyes of Von, Chloe, and Rosa, all of the issues and beef that existed between the two guys was effectively dead then and there. The girls both smiled at the same time and hugged one another. To them, that was a sign that Tito accepted the style of relationship they'd decided to embrace. But, Tito was a crafty and deceptive dude. He may had put up the appearance that he'd let everything go, but the thing he had in mind and at heart, was to get down to the bottom of any and all situations. Especially in his pursuit to know *exactly* who killed Alfredo.

Von's name was *not* scratched from the list of those suspected by Tito. At least not yet.

TO BE CONTINUED...

Lock Down Publications and Ca$h Presents
Assisted Publishing Packages

BASIC PACKAGE	UPGRADED PACKAGE
$499	$800
Editing	Typing
Cover Design	Editing
Formatting	Cover Design
	Formatting
ADVANCE PACKAGE	**LDP SUPREME PACKAGE**
$1,200	$1,500
Typing	Typing
Editing	Editing
Cover Design	Cover Design
Formatting	Formatting
Copyright registration	Copyright registration
Proofreading	Proofreading
Upload book to Amazon	Set up Amazon account
	Upload book to Amazon
	Advertise on LDP, Amazon and
	Facebook Page

***Other services available upon request.
Additional charges may apply

Lock Down Publications
P.O. Box 944
Stockbridge, GA 30281-9998
Phone: 470 303-9761

Submission Guideline

Submit the first three chapters of your completed manuscript to ldpsubmissions@gmail.com. In the subject line add **Your Book's Title**. The manuscript must be in a Word Doc file and sent as an attachment. Document should be in Times New Roman, double spaced, and in size 12 font. Also, provide your synopsis and full contact information. If sending multiple submissions, they must each be in a separate email.

Have a story but no way to send it electronically? You can still submit to LDP/Ca$h Presents. Send in the first three chapters, written or typed, of your completed manuscript to:

LDP: Submissions Dept
P.O. Box 944
Stockbridge, GA 30281-9998

DO NOT send original manuscript. Must be a duplicate.
Provide your synopsis and a cover letter containing your full contact information.

Thanks for considering LDP and Ca$h Presents.

NEW RELEASES

BLOODLINE OF A SAVAGE **BY PRINCE A. TAUHID**

THE MURDER QUEENS 4 **BY MICHAEL GALLON**

THE BUTTERFLY MAFIA **BY FUMIYA PAYNE**

KING KILLA 2 **BY VINCENT "VITTO" HOLLOWAY**

BABY, I'M WINTERTIME COLD 3 **BY MEESHA**

THESE VICIOUS STREETS **BY PRINCE A. TAUHID**

TIL DEATH 2 **BY ARYANNA**

CITY OF SMOKE 2 **BY MOLOTTI**

STEPPERS **BY KING RIO**

THE LANE **BY KEN-KEN SPENCE**

MONEY GAME 2 **BY SMOOVE DOLLA**

THE BLACK DIAMOND CARTEL **BY SAYNOMORE**

CRIME BOSS 2 **BY PLAYA RAY**

THUG OF SPADES **BY COREY ROBINSON**

LOVE IN THE TRENCHES 2 **BY COREY ROBINSON**

TIL DEATH 3 **BY ARYANNA**

THE BIRTH OF A GANGSTER 4 **BY DELMONT PLAYER**

PRODUCT OF THE STREETS **BY DEMOND "MONEY" ANDERSON**

Coming Soon from Lock Down Publications/Ca$h Presents

BLOOD OF A BOSS VI
SHADOWS OF THE GAME II
TRAP BASTARD II
By **Askari**

LOYAL TO THE GAME IV
By **T.J. & Jelissa**

TRUE SAVAGE VIII
MIDNIGHT CARTEL IV
DOPE BOY MAGIC IV
CITY OF KINGZ III
NIGHTMARE ON SILENT AVE II
THE PLUG OF LIL MEXICO II
CLASSIC CITY II
By **Chris Green**

BLAST FOR ME III
A SAVAGE DOPEBOY III
CUTTHROAT MAFIA III
DUFFLE BAG CARTEL VII
HEARTLESS GOON VI
By **Ghost**

A HUSTLER'S DECEIT III
KILL ZONE II
BAE BELONGS TO ME III
TIL DEATH II
By **Aryanna**

KING OF THE TRAP III
By **T.J. Edwards**

GORILLAZ IN THE BAY V
3X KRAZY III
STRAIGHT BEAST MODE III
By **De'Kari**

KINGPIN KILLAZ IV
STREET KINGS III
PAID IN BLOOD III
CARTEL KILLAZ IV
DOPE GODS III
By **Hood Rich**

SINS OF A HUSTLA II
By **ASAD**

YAYO V
BRED IN THE GAME 2
By **S. Allen**

THE STREETS WILL TALK II
By **Yolanda Moore**

SON OF A DOPE FIEND III
HEAVEN GOT A GHETTO III
SKI MASK MONEY III
By **Renta**

LOYALTY AIN'T PROMISED III
By **Keith Williams**

I'M NOTHING WITHOUT HIS LOVE II
SINS OF A THUG II
TO THE THUG I LOVED BEFORE II
IN A HUSTLER I TRUST II
By **Monet Dragun**

QUIET MONEY IV
EXTENDED CLIP III
THUG LIFE IV
By **Trai'Quan**

THE STREETS MADE ME IV
By **Larry D. Wright**

IF YOU CROSS ME ONCE III
ANGEL V
By **Anthony Fields**

THE STREETS WILL NEVER CLOSE IV
By **K'ajji**

HARD AND RUTHLESS III
KILLA KOUNTY IV
By **Khufu**

MONEY GAME III
By **Smoove Dolla**

MURDA WAS THE CASE III
Elijah R. Freeman

AN UNFORESEEN LOVE IV
BABY, I'M WINTERTIME COLD III
By **Meesha**

QUEEN OF THE ZOO III
By **Black Migo**

CONFESSIONS OF A JACKBOY III
By **Nicholas Lock**

JACK BOYS VS DOPE BOYS IV
A GANGSTA'S QUR'AN V
COKE GIRLZ II
COKE BOYS II
LIFE OF A SAVAGE V
CHI'RAQ GANGSTAS V
SOSA GANG III
BRONX SAVAGES II
BODYMORE KINGPINS II
By **Romell Tukes**

KING KILLA II
By **Vincent "Vitto" Holloway**

BETRAYAL OF A THUG III
By **Fre$h**

THE MURDER QUEENS III
By **Michael Gallon**

THE BIRTH OF A GANGSTER III
By **Delmont Player**

TREAL LOVE II
By **Le'Monica Jackson**

FOR THE LOVE OF BLOOD III
By **Jamel Mitchell**

RAN OFF ON DA PLUG II
By **Paper Boi Rari**

HOOD CONSIGLIERE III
By **Keese**

PRETTY GIRLS DO NASTY THINGS II
By **Nicole Goosby**

PROTÉGÉ OF A LEGEND III
LOVE IN THE TRENCHES II
By **Corey Robinson**

IT'S JUST ME AND YOU II
By **Ah'Million**

FOREVER GANGSTA III
By **Adrian Dulan**

GORILLAZ IN THE TRENCHES II
By **SayNoMore**

THE COCAINE PRINCESS VIII
By **King Rio**

CRIME BOSS II
By **Playa Ray**

LOYALTY IS EVERYTHING III
By **Molotti**

HERE TODAY GONE TOMORROW II
By **Fly Rock**

REAL G'S MOVE IN SILENCE II
By **Von Diesel**

GRIMEY WAYS IV
By **Ray Vinci**

Available Now

RESTRAINING ORDER I & II
By **CA$H & Coffee**

LOVE KNOWS NO BOUNDARIES I II & III
By **Coffee**

RAISED AS A GOON I, II, III & IV
BRED BY THE SLUMS I, II, III
BLAST FOR ME I & II
ROTTEN TO THE CORE I II III
A BRONX TALE I, II, III
DUFFLE BAG CARTEL I II III IV V VI
HEARTLESS GOON I II III IV V
A SAVAGE DOPEBOY I II
DRUG LORDS I II III
CUTTHROAT MAFIA I II
KING OF THE TRENCHES
By **Ghost**

LAY IT DOWN I & II
LAST OF A DYING BREED I II
BLOOD STAINS OF A SHOTTA I & II III
By **Jamaica**

LOYAL TO THE GAME I II III
LIFE OF SIN I, II III
By **TJ & Jelissa**

IF LOVING HIM IS WRONG…I & II
LOVE ME EVEN WHEN IT HURTS I II III
By **Jelissa**

BLOODY COMMAS I & II
SKI MASK CARTEL I, II & III
KING OF NEW YORK I II, III IV V
RISE TO POWER I II III
COKE KINGS I II III IV V
BORN HEARTLESS I II III IV
KING OF THE TRAP I II
By **T.J. Edwards**

WHEN THE STREETS CLAP BACK I & II III
THE HEART OF A SAVAGE I II III IV
MONEY MAFIA I II
LOYAL TO THE SOIL I II III
By **Jibril Williams**

A DISTINGUISHED THUG STOLE MY HEART I II &
III
LOVE SHOULDN'T HURT I II III IV
RENEGADE BOYS I II III IV
PAID IN KARMA I II III
SAVAGE STORMS I II III
AN UNFORESEEN LOVE I II III
BABY, I'M WINTERTIME COLD I II
By **Meesha**

A GANGSTER'S CODE I &, II III
A GANGSTER'S SYN I II III
THE SAVAGE LIFE I II III
CHAINED TO THE STREETS I II III
BLOOD ON THE MONEY I II III
A GANGSTA'S PAIN I II III
By **J-Blunt**

PUSH IT TO THE LIMIT
By **Bre' Hayes**

BLOOD OF A BOSS I, II, III, IV, V
SHADOWS OF THE GAME
TRAP BASTARD
By **Askari**

THE STREETS BLEED MURDER I, II & III
THE HEART OF A GANGSTA I II& III
By **Jerry Jackson**

CUM FOR ME I II III IV V VI VII VIII
An **LDP Erotica Collaboration**

BRIDE OF A HUSTLA I II & II
THE FETTI GIRLS I, II& III
CORRUPTED BY A GANGSTA I, II III, IV
BLINDED BY HIS LOVE
THE PRICE YOU PAY FOR LOVE I, II ,III
DOPE GIRL MAGIC I II III
By **Destiny Skai**

WHEN A GOOD GIRL GOES BAD
By **Adrienne**

A GANGSTER'S REVENGE I II III & IV
THE BOSS MAN'S DAUGHTERS I II III IV V
A SAVAGE LOVE I & II
BAE BELONGS TO ME I II
A HUSTLER'S DECEIT I, II, III
WHAT BAD BITCHES DO I, II, III
SOUL OF A MONSTER I II III
KILL ZONE
A DOPE BOY'S QUEEN I II III
TIL DEATH
By **Aryanna**

THE COST OF LOYALTY I II III
By Kweli

A KINGPIN'S AMBITION
A KINGPIN'S AMBITION **II**
I MURDER FOR THE DOUGH
By **Ambitious**

TRUE SAVAGE I II III IV V VI VII
DOPE BOY MAGIC I, II, III
MIDNIGHT CARTEL I II III
CITY OF KINGZ I II
NIGHTMARE ON SILENT AVE
THE PLUG OF LIL MEXICO II
CLASSIC CITY
By **Chris Green**

A DOPEBOY'S PRAYER
By **Eddie "Wolf" Lee**

THE KING CARTEL I, II & III
By **Frank Gresham**

THESE NIGGAS AIN'T LOYAL I, II & III
By **Nikki Tee**

GANGSTA SHYT I II &III
By **CATO**

THE ULTIMATE BETRAYAL
By **Phoenix**

BOSS'N UP I, II & III
By **Royal Nicole**

I LOVE YOU TO DEATH
By **Destiny J**

I RIDE FOR MY HITTA
I STILL RIDE FOR MY HITTA
By **Misty Holt**

LOVE & CHASIN' PAPER
By **Qay Crockett**

TO DIE IN VAIN
SINS OF A HUSTLA
By **ASAD**

BROOKLYN HUSTLAZ
By **Boogsy Morina**

BROOKLYN ON LOCK I & II
By **Sonovia**

GANGSTA CITY
By **Teddy Duke**

A DRUG KING AND HIS DIAMOND I & II III
A DOPEMAN'S RICHES
HER MAN, MINE'S TOO I, II
CASH MONEY HO'S
THE WIFEY I USED TO BE I II
PRETTY GIRLS DO NASTY THINGS
By Nicole Goosby

LIPSTICK KILLAH I, II, III
CRIME OF PASSION I II & III
FRIEND OR FOE I II III
By **Mimi**

TRAPHOUSE KING I II & III
KINGPIN KILLAZ I II III
STREET KINGS I II
PAID IN BLOOD I II
CARTEL KILLAZ I II III
DOPE GODS I II
By **Hood Rich**

STEADY MOBBN' I, II, III
THE STREETS STAINED MY SOUL I II III
By **Marcellus Allen**

WHO SHOT YA I, II, III
SON OF A DOPE FIEND I II
HEAVEN GOT A GHETTO I II
SKI MASK MONEY I II
By **Renta**

GORILLAZ IN THE BAY I II III IV
TEARS OF A GANGSTA I II
3X KRAZY I II
STRAIGHT BEAST MODE I II
By **DE'KARI**

TRIGGADALE I II III
MURDA WAS THE CASE I II
By **Elijah R. Freeman**

THE STREETS ARE CALLING
By **Duquie Wilson**

SLAUGHTER GANG I II III
RUTHLESS HEART I II III
By **Willie Slaughter**

GOD BLESS THE TRAPPERS I, II, III
THESE SCANDALOUS STREETS I, II, III
FEAR MY GANGSTA I, II, III IV, V
THESE STREETS DON'T LOVE NOBODY I, II
BURY ME A G I, II, III, IV, V
A GANGSTA'S EMPIRE I, II, III, IV
THE DOPEMAN'S BODYGAURD I II
THE REALEST KILLAZ I II III
THE LAST OF THE OGS I II III
By **Tranay Adams**

MARRIED TO A BOSS I II III
By **Destiny Skai & Chris Green**

KINGZ OF THE GAME I II III IV V VI VII
CRIME BOSS
By **Playa Ray**

FUK SHYT
By **Blakk Diamond**

DON'T F#CK WITH MY HEART I II
By **Linnea**

ADDICTED TO THE DRAMA I II III
IN THE ARM OF HIS BOSS II
By **Jamila**

YAYO I II III IV
A SHOOTER'S AMBITION I II
BRED IN THE GAME
By **S. Allen**

LOYALTY AIN'T PROMISED I II
By **Keith Williams**

TRAP GOD I II III
RICH $AVAGE I II III
MONEY IN THE GRAVE I II III
By **Martell Troublesome Bolden**

FOREVER GANGSTA I II
GLOCKS ON SATIN SHEETS I II
By **Adrian Dulan**

TOE TAGZ I II III IV
LEVELS TO THIS SHYT I II
IT'S JUST ME AND YOU
By **Ah'Million**

KINGPIN DREAMS I II III
RAN OFF ON DA PLUG
By **Paper Boi Rari**

CONFESSIONS OF A GANGSTA I II III IV
CONFESSIONS OF A JACKBOY I II
By **Nicholas Lock**

I'M NOTHING WITHOUT HIS LOVE
SINS OF A THUG
TO THE THUG I LOVED BEFORE
A GANGSTA SAVED XMAS
IN A HUSTLER I TRUST
By **Monet Dragun**

QUIET MONEY I II III
THUG LIFE I II III
EXTENDED CLIP I II
A GANGSTA'S PARADISE
By **Trai'Quan**

CAUGHT UP IN THE LIFE I II III
THE STREETS NEVER LET GO I II III
By **Robert Baptiste**

NEW TO THE GAME I II III
MONEY, MURDER & MEMORIES I II III
By **Malik D. Rice**

CREAM I II III
THE STREETS WILL TALK
By **Yolanda Moore**

LIFE OF A SAVAGE I II III IV
A GANGSTA'S QUR'AN I II III IV
MURDA SEASON I II III
GANGLAND CARTEL I II III
CHI'RAQ GANGSTAS I II III IV
KILLERS ON ELM STREET I II III
JACK BOYZ N DA BRONX I II III
A DOPEBOY'S DREAM I II III
JACK BOYS VS DOPE BOYS I II III
COKE GIRLZ
COKE BOYS
SOSA GANG I II
BRONX SAVAGES
BODYMORE KINGPINS
By **Romell Tukes**

THE STREETS MADE ME I II III
By **Larry D. Wright**

CONCRETE KILLA I II III
VICIOUS LOYALTY I II III
By **Kingpen**

THE ULTIMATE SACRIFICE I, II, III, IV, V, VI
KHADIFI
IF YOU CROSS ME ONCE I II
ANGEL I II III IV
IN THE BLINK OF AN EYE
By **Anthony Fields**

THE LIFE OF A HOOD STAR
By **Ca$h & Rashia Wilson**

THE STREETS WILL NEVER CLOSE I II III
By **K'ajji**

NIGHTMARES OF A HUSTLA I II III
By **King Dream**

HARD AND RUTHLESS I II
MOB TOWN 251
THE BILLIONAIRE BENTLEYS I II III
REAL G'S MOVE IN SILENCE
By **Von Diesel**

GHOST MOB
By **Stilloan Robinson**

MOB TIES I II III IV V VI
SOUL OF A HUSTLER, HEART OF A KILLER I II
GORILLAZ IN THE TRENCHES
By **SayNoMore**

BODYMORE MURDERLAND I II III
THE BIRTH OF A GANGSTER I II
By **Delmont Player**

FOR THE LOVE OF A BOSS
By **C. D. Blue**

KILLA KOUNTY I II III IV
By Khufu

MOBBED UP I II III IV
THE BRICK MAN I II III IV V
THE COCAINE PRINCESS I II III IV V VI VII
By **King Rio**

MONEY GAME I II
By **Smoove Dolla**

A GANGSTA'S KARMA I II III
By **FLAME**

KING OF THE TRENCHES I II III
By **GHOST & TRANAY ADAMS**

QUEEN OF THE ZOO I II
By **Black Migo**

GRIMEY WAYS I II III
By **Ray Vinci**

XMAS WITH AN ATL SHOOTER
By **Ca$h & Destiny Skai**

KING KILLA
By **Vincent "Vitto" Holloway**

BETRAYAL OF A THUG I II
By **Fre$h**

BLOODLINE OF A SAVAGE II | PRINCE A. TAUHID

THE MURDER QUEENS I II
By **Michael Gallon**

TREAL LOVE
By **Le'Monica Jackson**

FOR THE LOVE OF BLOOD I II
By **Jamel Mitchell**

HOOD CONSIGLIERE I II
By **Keese**

PROTÉGÉ OF A LEGEND I II
LOVE IN THE TRENCHES
By **Corey Robinson**

BORN IN THE GRAVE I II III
By **Self Made Tay**

MOAN IN MY MOUTH
By **XTASY**

TORN BETWEEN A GANGSTER AND A
GENTLEMAN
By **J-BLUNT & Miss Kim**

LOYALTY IS EVERYTHING I II
By **Molotti**

HERE TODAY GONE TOMORROW
By **Fly Rock**

PILLOW PRINCESS
By **S. Hawkins**

SANCTIFIED AND HORNY
by **XTASY**

THE PLUG OF LIL MEXICO 2
by **CHRIS GREEN**

THE BLACK DIAMOND CARTEL
by **SAYNOMORE**

THE BIRTH OF A GANGSTER 3
by **DELMONT PLAYER**

BOOKS BY LDP'S CEO, CA$H

TRUST IN NO MAN
TRUST IN NO MAN 2
TRUST IN NO MAN 3
BONDED BY BLOOD
SHORTY GOT A THUG
THUGS CRY
THUGS CRY 2
THUGS CRY 3
TRUST NO BITCH
TRUST NO BITCH 2
TRUST NO BITCH 3
TIL MY CASKET DROPS
RESTRAINING ORDER
RESTRAINING ORDER 2
IN LOVE WITH A CONVICT
LIFE OF A HOOD STAR
XMAS WITH AN ATL SHOOTER